...ed, and he stood stock-still, watching closely as the little mound of earth began to grow. He bent down. 'Come on, moley,' he whispered. 'I won't hurt you.'

All at once the hill erupted and out came – not a cute, velvety mole – but a hand!

Bony and hairy, the hand grasped at the air like some hideous mutant meat-eating plant. Once. Twice. The third time it struck lucky and, with the boy's wrist in its grasp, it squeezed viciously.

Sam screamed. His blood turned to ice. He tore at the fingers with his free hand, horrified by their strength. 'Let me go!' he said through gritted teeth. 'Let me GO!'

Haunted by nightmares of the terrifying Tom Tiddler, Sam dreads going to sleep each night. But then, when Tom Tiddler starts to appear to him in the day-time too, Sam realizes that it isn't just a character from a bad dream he's dealing with – something far more terrifying has been woken. . .

THE WAKENING

Paul Stewart

CORGI YEARLING BOOKS

THE WAKENING
A CORGI YEARLING BOOK : 0 440 86347 3

First publication in Great Britain

PRINTING HISTORY
Yearling edition published 1996
Reissued 1999

Set in 12/14½pt Linotype New Century Schoolbook by
Phoenix Typesetting, Ilkley, West Yorkshire

Corgi Yearling Books are published by Transworld Publishers Ltd,
61–63 Uxbridge Road, Ealing, London W5 5SA,
in Australia by Transworld Publishers,
c/o Random House Australia Pty. Ltd,
20 Alfred Street, Milsons Point, NSW 2061,
and in New Zealand by Transworld Publishers,
c/o Random House New Zealand,
18 Poland Road, Glenfield, Auckland.

Made and printed in Great Britain by
Cox & Wyman Ltd, Reading, Berkshire

For Joseph and Anna

CHAPTER ONE

Sam curled up under the duvet. 'Don't let me have the nightmare again,' he whispered. 'Not tonight.'

The following day was the first of the new term and Sam needed a good night's sleep. He was going up into Mr Cooper's class – the top class at Rowgate Middle – and he didn't want to feel tired all day.

The clock was ticking. The central heating was humming. Cars hissed by on the wet road outside. And the whole lot all mixed up together nicely in a warm, familiar drone.

Suddenly, Sam started. There was another noise. A noise that was just as familiar, but not half so nice. His parents were arguing. Again!

Sam wrapped his pillow around his head. It muffled the voices, but didn't shut them out completely.

'Stop it,' he said quietly. 'Just stop it.'

Sam wanted to go downstairs and give them both a great big hug. But he'd tried that once before, and it hadn't worked. Angry with each other, they'd both simply turned that anger on him.

'Get back to bed at once!' his mum had shouted.

'And don't let me catch you down here again,' yelled his dad.

No, when they were in this sort of mood, it was best to keep out of their way. Anyway, his dad would be going out soon. Sam rolled onto his back, put his hands behind his head and stared up at the ceiling.

He thought of Mr Cooper. Everyone said he was nice enough when you got to know him. Firm but fair! So long as he didn't have to sit too near Craig Martin – they'd never got on! – Sam knew that he'd be just fine.

So why was he worried? Why did that first day back at school always make him so nervous? Sam sighed. He knew the answer, of course. It was change.

Sam hated change. Any change at all. He liked things to stay just the way they were.

At that moment, the voices downstairs became so loud that every single word rang out, crystal clear.

'Because we can't afford it,' his dad roared.

'I am not having him going to school looking like some street urchin,' his mum screamed back.

Sam felt his stomach knotting. Money, again! It was the cause of all his parents' rows. Ever since his dad had been made redundant, money – or rather, the lack of it – had taken over their lives. Mum still had her part-time job at the supermarket, and Dad did some night-time taxi work. But it just wasn't enough. The house saw to that.

Three years earlier, they had moved into what Sam's mum and dad had called their 'dream-house'. Situated in the middle of town, it was well over a hundred years old, and still contained most of its original features. 'We'll do it up,' his dad had said. 'It'll be perfect,' said his mum. But then, as the money problems started, so the renovations stopped. The dream-house had become a nightmare.

'We'll have to tighten our belts,' Dad had said.

And tighten them, they had. At dinner-time, succulent pork and beef was more often than not replaced by nourishing lentils and beans. That summer, for the first time since Sam could remember, they hadn't gone on holiday. And when the video broke, it had stayed broken.

Sam could put up with all this. He could even cope with Craig Martin taking the mickey out of his cheap trainers. What he couldn't bear was his parents arguing about him.

CHAPTER TWO

In a dark place, not so very far away, something stirred. Something no longer of this world. Something that no longer even knew what it was.

What can *we* call it then, this 'something'? A spirit? A ghost? A ghoul? A phantom? Once it had been a man, that much is certain. But now? What name is there for a multitude of swirling atoms held together by the past? A memory? Yes, perhaps that is the best word . . .

Deep down under the ground, in a pocket of dank air, the memory stirred.

It had been asleep for a hundred years. And so it should have remained – so it *would* have remained, if it hadn't been for the smell.

For the seventh time in as many weeks, the memory quivered as a familiar odour seeped down through the earth. It squirmed and writhed as the smell brought back distant scenes best left forgotten.

For of all the senses, it is smell which can best awaken the memory. Sight and sound soon forget, and taste can too easily be tricked. As for touch, it is not developed enough in any but the blind. But smell! The faintest scent sets your nostrils twitching and takes you back to places you once knew: your first classroom; your grandmother's kitchen; a certain wood, on a certain day.

Tonight, the smell was more pungent than ever. What was more, it was now complete. Before, it had been familiar enough to trouble the sleeping memory, but not sufficient to wake it. Something had been missing. Tonight was different. Tonight the smell was tinged with something new. Something familiar, which was filtering down into the underground chamber. Tonight something was going to happen.

CHAPTER THREE

'If only *I* could get hold of some money,' Sam said to himself, as he wiped away his tears angrily. 'It can't be *that* difficult.'

And while his mum and dad kept at it, hammer and tongs, downstairs, Sam imagined himself walking into a bank. He was wearing a balaclava helmet, sunglasses, a false moustache. His collar was up.

He strode over to the counter and slipped a note to the cashier. She looked up, surprised.

'Ten thousand pounds?' she said.

Sam nodded. 'And hurry up about it!' he said, as gruffly as he could.

The woman looked down at his note. ' "Or I'll skoot!" ' she read. She looked up. 'Skoot?'

'Shoot!' Sam hissed.

'Pardon?' said the cashier.

'Shoot,' said Sam. He pushed his finger hard against the lining of his pocket and pointed it over the counter. 'I've got a gun!'

BANG!

Sam jumped. His brain struggled to make sense of the sudden noise. Had the police arrived and opened fire? Had his own gun gone off? No, it couldn't have, he remembered. He only had a finger!

Had *that* gone off?

The next moment, there was a second bang. A quieter one, this time. The sound of a car door being slammed. A taxi door, to be precise. His dad had left for work.

Sam opened his eyes and looked around the room. He must have dropped off.

He was rubbing away the pins and needles in his hands when he caught sight of a shadow on the landing. The next moment his mum's head appeared in the doorway.

'Hello,' she said, surprised. 'Aren't you asleep yet?'

'Something woke me,' said Sam.

'The front door slamming, I expect,' she said. 'You know what it's like when the wind gets up.'

Sam nodded. 'Dad wasn't angry, then?' he said.

'Angry?' his mum said, a little vaguely.

14

'Yes,' said Sam, beginning to get irritated. 'You know. Cross. Shouting. That sort of thing.'

His mum sighed. The light from the landing made deep shadows of the lines on her face. She looked older than Sam had ever seen her before.

'That interview your dad had with Morleys,' she said wearily. 'He didn't get the job. And they're talking about laying off the part-timers at the supermarket. I just don't know what we're going to do.' She looked away.

'Things are bound to get better,' said Sam, trying to sound confident and mature. 'You'll see.'

His mum squeezed his hands. 'You're a good boy,' she said. 'Best boy! Now, turn over and go back to sleep,' she said, as she got up. 'You've got a long day ahead of you.'

Sam looked up at her. 'I'm frightened of getting the nightmare again,' he said.

'Oh, Sam!' said his mum. 'Is that still bothering you?'

Sam nodded. The lump in his throat was coming back.

'And you still can't remember what it's about?'

'No,' he said. 'It disappears when I wake up. I just get left with the feel of it. The *taste* of it. Dirty. Rotten.' Sam shuddered. 'Metallic.'

His mum sat down again, and began stroking his temple with her thumb. 'The trick is to go to sleep thinking of something nice. What would you like to dream about tonight?' she said softly.

Sam closed his eyes. 'Playing football . . . no, cricket,' he said. 'Over at the park. With Danno and Waz and . . .' His voice trailed away.

'What else?' whispered his mum.

'Ice cream,' he said. 'The biggest Ninety-Nine in the world! With chocolate sauce . . . And chopped nuts . . .'

The stroking continued. Warm and soft. Sam felt himself growing drowsier and drowsier.

'And hundreds and thousands . . .' he murmured.

For a split second, the thumb stopped moving. When it started up again the stroking was slightly jerkier, a little bit more hurried. On Sam's face, at least, there was no sign that he had even noticed. But as he finally drifted off to sleep, Sam was wondering how he would ever *pay* for such an enormous ice cream.

'N'night, love,' said his mum, as she kissed him on the cheek. 'Sweet dreams!'

CHAPTER FOUR

For a while at least, it seemed as if his mum's idea was working. Sam found himself at the park, playing cricket with Waz, Danno and some other friends – just as he'd wanted. What was more, he'd just hit the ball for a brilliant six.

As Sam watched Gopher chasing after it, he heard a familiar plinkety-plinkety sound. It was the Mr Smoothy van!

'He's over there,' Waz yelled, and pointed to the red and blue vehicle on the far side of the park. 'Come on!'

Without another word, all six boys were racing across the grass towards the promise of a Ninety-Nine. Suddenly, Sam stopped.

'Idiot!' he muttered.

His money was in his jacket, and his jacket was rolled up in a bundle behind the wicket.

'I'll catch you up,' he yelled to the others, as he spun round and belted back to the heap of clothes.

But even as he said the words, Sam knew that he'd made a dreadful mistake. *It* was happening again, and Sam's heart began to thump with fearful anticipation.

He knew that he should have stuck with the others. Danno could have lent him the money – he always had loads on him. But now it was too late. He had become separated from the others just as he *always* became separated from them. That was the way the nightmare worked. Luring him. Lulling him into a false sense of security. And ensnaring him.

Sam looked around. The pitch, the stumps, the pile of jackets; they had all disappeared.

Instead, he was standing in the middle of a dark, silent forest, choked with dense under-growth. Not an animal stirred. Not a bird sang.

CHAPTER FIVE

In the darkness, the memory was growing stronger. Filled with the intoxicating smell, it tossed and turned, trying to waken.

The smell itself was a curious mixture of sweet perfume and sour decay. An odd smell. A smell it is difficult to describe.

There is a fruit in the East called the durian. Eating it, so travellers say, is like eating strawberries in a sewer. Such was the smell which now filled the underground chamber. An aromatic odour. A fragrant stench which once smelt, could never be forgotten.

Slowly, the memory began to take shape. The atoms coalesced. The past congealed. Lovers of the durian claim that even the faintest smell of the fruit will make their mouths water. So it was with the memory. As the smell grew more powerful, saliva flowed once more in its mouth and blood began to pump through its veins.

It stretched. It yawned. The eyes snapped open and the being it had once again become stared blindly into the blackness. For a second it was confused. And then it remembered. The smell had done its work, and the memory of what had happened was as clear as if it had happened only yesterday.

The creature opened its mouth, and howled. 'NOOOOOOO!'

CHAPTER SIX

Sam's dad was tired. The night had started busily enough, but it was almost two in the morning now, and Pete Dillon hadn't had anyone in his taxi for over an hour.

'No-one wants to go out on a night like this,' he said to himself. 'All tucked up in bed, I 'spect. Snug and warm.' And he thought longingly of his own bed – and his wife asleep in it.

He leant forward and switched the car stereo on. A country-and-western song filled the taxi with the story of a broken heart. The sloppy lyrics brought a lump to his throat.

'I'm sorry, love,' he murmured. 'I'm sorry, Sam. Again!'

Just then, the radio crackled, and the song

faded away into static. Pete looked down irritably. Seconds passed, and the hissing remained. He twiddled the knob. Nothing. He switched it off-on-off-on. Still nothing. Finally he hit it. That didn't work either.

'Typical!' he grunted, and chose a cassette instead. 'Get in, you little so-and-so,' he said. 'Get in!'

But the cassette would not go in. The heavy blow had buckled the front of the machine and, when Pete had pushed the cassette into the slot, it had got stuck. Completely stuck. It wouldn't go in and it wouldn't come out.

Leaning over, he looked more closely at the machine. He fingered the v-shape of bent metal, and sighed.

Pete Dillon knew that he lost his temper too quickly. He always had – not that that made it any better. And when he did, he broke things. Car stereos. Families.

Out of the static came the sound of violins and slide guitars. The country-and-western song was back. Pete smiled.

'I'll try harder from now on,' he promised. 'I will.'

The song was interrupted abruptly for a second time. This time by the nasal, sing-song voice of Sheila back at base.

'Car twenty-seven, can you confirm your position? Over.'

22

Pete picked up his handset and pressed the button. 'Brookes Road. Over.'

'Airport job for you, if you're interested, car twenty-seven. Over.'

Airport? Pete thought. Fifty quid at this time of the night. 'I *am* interested. Over,' he said.

'The customer's at number sixt . . .'

Pete listened in disbelief as the address disappeared on a wave of crackle.

'Come in, base,' he said. 'I'm not reading you. Come in, base. Come in, base. Sheila, don't do this to me!'

But there was nothing. Only crackle. What was more, the radio was hissing once again. He leant back in his seat.

'I don't believe it,' he muttered. 'I do not believe it! What the hell is going on tonight?'

CHAPTER SEVEN

Sam stumbled on through the dense under-growth. His heart was pounding, his teeth were chattering.

'Why am I here again?' he wailed. 'Why?'

The question was lost in the swirling mist. Yet it was not all silence. There was *something* there. Sam kept perfectly still. Yes. There it was again. Something new. The sound of voices. Children's voices chanting a rhyme.

'Danno!' Sam yelled. 'Gopher, Waz . . . Don't move! I'm coming to find you.' And with that, he raced off towards his friends. Scratched by brambles and tripped by gnarled roots, Sam stumbled on. 'Just don't go silent on me,' he panted.

But the rhyme showed no sign of stopping. As his friends became more and more excited with their game, their voices rang out through the forest, loud and clear. Except . . . Sam trembled. Except . . . Shivers of dark foreboding zigzagged up and down his spine. He stopped running, and listened.

Those weren't his friends at all! Their voices were too young – and some of them were girls. 'A trap,' he gasped. 'I've got to go back.'

But by now, of course, it was too late. At that very moment, Sam found himself stepping into a clearing.

Nothing – nothing at all was growing in it. 'Weird,' said Sam. 'As if the earth's been poisoned, or burned . . .' He looked all round him. 'In a big circle.'

At that moment, Sam heard the children again. They were giggling, sniggering, squealing with excitement. Sam peered in vain into the surrounding undergrowth.

'Where are you?' he shouted angrily. 'Show your faces!'

The children would not.

'You're IT!' one of them cried.

'But I don't know what the game is,' Sam said. His heart was pumping. His knees were beginning to shake. 'What am I supposed to do?' he yelled.

Instead of replying, the children took up their chant once more.

'Here we are in Tom Tiddler's Ground
Picking up gold and silver.'

'Gold and silver?' said Sam, looking around wildly. 'Where?'

As his eyes darted about the clearing, he saw that there was something even stranger about the circular clearing than he had first noticed. Not only was nothing growing, but the bare earth had been stained different colours, like a target. There was an outer ring of dark brown earth, which bordered on the forest. An inner ring of grey earth. And within this, a smaller circle of black earth.

Then Sam saw it. Lying at the dead centre of the bullseye, was a shiny silver coin.

'Quick!' shouted one of the boys from his hiding place.

'Take it – and RUN!' cried one of the girls.

Sam tiptoed towards the coin. His mouth was dry. His legs felt weak. He crossed into the black circle, stopped and reached down. Slowly, his fingers closed around the piece of silver.

'Get out of there!' the children yelled. 'Now!'

But Sam was deaf to their urgent pleas. He was concentrating on something else he'd heard. Something close by. A sort of scrabbling sound.

He looked down. The earth by his feet was moving.

'A mole.' Sam smiled, and he stood stock-still, watching closely as the little mound of earth began to grow. He bent down. 'Come on, moley,' he whispered, 'I won't hurt you.'

All at once the hill erupted and out came – not a cute, velvety mole – but a hand!

Bony and hairy, the hand grasped at the air like some hideous mutant meat-eating plant. Once. Twice. The third time it struck lucky and, with the boy's wrist in its grasp, it squeezed viciously.

Sam screamed. His blood turned to ice. He tore at the fingers with his free hand, horrified by their strength. 'Let me go!' he said through gritted teeth. 'Let me GO!'

In desperation, Sam struggled and tugged. The silver coin dropped to the ground. But still the hand would not release its ferocious grip.

'Help me!' Sam cried out to beyond the circle. But there was no reply. The boys and girls had all disappeared. Sam was alone.

What could he do? Pulling free was impossible, that much was clear.

'Twist yourself free,' he said to himself, and started walking round in a circle, waiting for the moment when the hand could twist no further.

But the moment never came. In horrified

disbelief, Sam realized that the hand was turning with him. He stopped. At least he tried to, but the hand kept turning.

Round and round, Sam was dragged against his will. Faster and faster – until, with a sudden jerk, his feet left the ground, and he found himself whirling round through the air. And as he spun, he heard a voice whispering into his ear.

'So near, and yet so far
Driven here by your ma and pa.
So far and yet so near
You'll *always* find a welcome here.'

With that, the hand abruptly released its grip, and Sam flew backwards. He landed with a bump on the outermost ring of the clearing, looked up, and stared at the hand. It was waving.

Sam could stand no more. He leapt to his feet and began running.

And he ran and ran and ran, not once daring to look back. Through the forest, jumping streams, over stiles and across field after field. He didn't stop. He couldn't stop.

His legs ached and tears were streaming down his face. But he had to get as far away as possible. He had to escape.

CHAPTER EIGHT

Sam was still crying when he woke up – or rather, he thought he was. When he finally opened his eyes, he realized that there were no tears. It was sweat pouring down his face.

Bewildered, he lay there for a moment. The smell of burnt toast wafted up from the kitchen.

'Smoke,' said Sam quietly. 'Something was burning. And there was . . .' But the nightmare was already fading fast. Just like it always did.

And yet, as he washed, dressed and had his breakfast, Sam grew more and more convinced that this time there *was* something there, up in his head. If he could just . . .

'A name!' he said suddenly.

'Pardon?' said his mum, looking up.

Sam realized he'd been thinking aloud. 'I . . . er . . . I was just wondering what day we'll have *games*,' he said, getting up from the table. 'I'd better be off,' he said.

'All right, then, love,' she said. 'Have a lovely day.'

As she watched her son leaving the house, Sally Dillon's smile disappeared. He really did need a new jacket. The one he was wearing looked horribly uncomfortable around the armpits.

'I'll get you a new one, Sam,' she whispered. 'If it's the last thing that I do.'

As he set off along the familiar route to school, the jacket was the last thing on Sam's mind.

The point is, he was thinking, why would I remember that there was a name, if it wasn't important? He turned right at the end of his road. It *must* be important, he concluded. In fact, if I could just think of it, I bet I'd never have the nightmare again. He kicked at a stone angrily. So what *is* it?

Trying, literally, to jog his memory, Sam jerked his head forward. 'It was. . . *unnh*!' he said, thrusting his neck forward in an attempt to dislodge the name from wherever it was hiding in his brain. 'It was . . . *unnh*!'

Nothing! He tried again. And again.

As he jerked his way along the pavement, with

30

his arms – forced out to the side by the tight jacket – flapping by his sides, Sam looked like nothing so much as a demented pigeon. And still the name refused to be remembered.

Sam stopped jerking. Unfortunately not quite soon enough. He had already been spotted.

'Oy! Don't stop!' came a voice. A horribly familiar voice.

Sam looked round. There on the other side of the road was Craig Martin and two of his cronies. All three of them were strutting along the road, thrusting their jaws out with every second step!

'Blast!' Sam muttered to himself. Trust Craig Martin to catch him acting like a nutter. He'd never hear the end of it. What a great way to start the term!

Head down, Sam increased his pace. But it was hopeless. Craig, Billy and Niall were already dodging the traffic as they crossed the road. The next moment, Sam found himself surrounded by the three boys.

'Pick up some horrible twitching disease, did you?' Craig sneered.

Sam took no notice. He tried to get past. But Craig hopped back, and bent over, pretending to have a hump.

'Unclean, unclean!' he shouted, and rang an imaginary bell in his face.

Sam pushed the hand away. Craig put it back.

31

Sam pushed it away again. Harder. The situation was threatening to get out of control. Behind him, Sam could hear Billy and Niall joining in – just as he knew they would. They copied everything Craig did.

'Leave me alone,' said Sam as, for the third time, he pushed away the hand which was waving under his nose.

Craig suddenly stopped. His big fists clenched. 'Watch it!' he warned, through tight lips.

Sam looked up. He noticed that Craig had that look in his eye. He was unpredictable at the best of times, but when he got *that* look, Craig Martin was dangerous.

'I . . . I . . .' Sam stuttered.

'I don't like being pushed,' said Craig. 'Understand?' He poked Sam viciously in the chest. 'Understand?'

Sam nodded. 'Who does?' he said quietly.

Craig stood back and folded his arms. 'Your mum packed you a nice little treat, has she?' he said.

Sam sighed. Here we go again, he thought as he rummaged in his bag. Every day, Sam's mum would pack him a certain little something to have with his milk, and every day, that certain little something – Mars bar, Kitkat, Twix, whatever – would end up in Craig Martin's stomach.

Sam wasn't the only one who suffered from Craig's chocolate racket. On a good day, Craig could extort and consume more chocolate than most children have in a month. He had the teeth to prove it.

'A Bounty,' said Sam, as he pulled the chocolate bar from his lunch box.

'That'll do nicely,' said Craig, and smiled.

It was an odd smile, with the lips stretched over the teeth. Craig had perfected it some time earlier. He thought it made him look hard. It did. But Craig had another reason for concealing his teeth. Every single one of them was brown and stubby, rotten to the core.

Sam was zipping up his bag when he heard footsteps running up behind him. All four boys turned to look. It was Waz.

'You heard the news?' he said excitedly.

'What news?' said Craig, through a mouthful of chocolate and coconut.

'It was on the telly this morning,' said Waz. 'Something jammed all the transmission signals in the night. Radio, police messages, telly . . . They reckon it could be . . .' Waz paused dramatically, 'aliens.'

Billy and Niall burst out laughing. Craig snorted with derision. He wanted to make it clear what *he* thought about the existence of aliens. Unfortunately, as he snorted, a lump of coconut shot down his throat the wrong way. He started coughing noisily.

'Back . . .' he spluttered.

'Back?' said Billy and Niall, and looked at one another in confusion.

'Back . . .' Craig gasped. Red-faced and bent double by the side of the road, Craig twisted his arm behind him and pointed to his back.

'I think he wants you to hit him on the back,' said Sam, trying hard not to grin.

'*Hit* him?' said Billy.

'Hit *Craig*?' said Niall.

Craig was nodding furiously.

'I think so,' said Sam.

Billy went round the front of Craig and crouched down. 'You want me to hit you on the back?' he said.

Craig's coughing was worse than ever. He could hardly breathe. He nodded that yes, he did want Billy to hit him on the back. And soon!

'You won't hit me back, will you?' said Billy, thinking it best to get things sorted now.

Somehow Craig managed to shake his head. Billy looked at his friend's purple face – getting him to promise was probably going *too* far. He went round to Craig's back and raised his hand.

'Come on,' said Sam to Waz.

As they walked off, they heard the thump of Billy's hand landing on Craig's back. Craig coughed one last cough – the coconut was out – and began gulping at the air greedily.

Waz turned round. 'He seems all right,' he said.

Craig's eyes were bloodshot and watery. Suddenly, he turned on Billy and punched him in the chest.

'What's that for?' Billy whined. 'You said you wouldn't hit me back.'

'I'm not hitting you *back*,' said Craig, punching him a second time. 'I'm hitting you 'cos you took so long. Divet!'

'Yeah, completely back to normal,' Waz sighed. 'Worse luck!'

'So what was all that about aliens, then?' said Sam.

Waz suddenly perked up again. 'Like I told you,' he said. 'There was some strange electrical force all over the town last night, and it jammed all the radio signals. No-one knows what could have caused it.'

'And they talked about aliens on the news?' said Sam.

'Yeah! Well . . . No, not exactly,' said Waz.

Sam groaned. 'What *did* they say exactly?'

'They said that they weren't ruling anything out. Anything!' he repeated meaningfully.

'Which means,' he continued, 'that they're still ruling everything in. Which means,' he concluded, 'that it could be aliens.'

As they reached the school gates, Sam looked at his friend. He was feeling oddly uneasy. 'Maybe,' he said.

CHAPTER NINE

The playground was still buzzing with the news of the radio interference when the bell went for morning register. And, as they made their way to their new classroom and picked where they were going to sit, the boys and girls of 8C continued to come up with more and more bizarre explanations.

'Perhaps a dinosaur bit through the power cables,' said one.

'Maybe a time machine made by a mad professor blocked out all other radio signals,' said another.

Waz was still of the opinion that aliens were to blame. Sam was keeping an open mind.

Seeing Danno sitting on his own on the right-hand side of the class, Sam immediately made a bee-line for the spare seat next to him. Not only was Danno rich, he was also big. Bigger than Craig Martin. Whenever Sam was with Danno, Craig steered clear of him.

'Anyone sitting here?' asked Sam.

Danno grinned. 'I was hoping that new girl might,' he said, looking round. 'But she's found somewhere else.'

'New girl?' said Sam, following Danno's gaze. She was on the other side of the classroom, sitting next to Elaine Pritchard. She looked nice. 'What's her name?' he said.

Danno shrugged.

At that moment, Mr Cooper came into the room.

'Morning, class,' he said.

'Morning, Mr Cooper,' everyone chanted back. Everyone, that is, except for Waz, whose mind was still elsewhere.

'Morning, Mrs Reynolds,' he said.

Everyone laughed. Mr Cooper stared at the boy in silence, waiting for him to look up. But Waz continued to stare down at the table top, unaware that everyone was looking at him.

'Er-hem,' Mr Cooper said loudly.

Waz finally lifted his eyes. He saw the new teacher glaring at him, and his face turned beetroot red.

'Sorry, sir,' he said.

Mr Cooper nodded sternly. 'Register,' he said. As Mr Cooper read through the names, both Sam and Danno listened carefully to find out what the new girl was called.

'. . . Paula Janning,' said Mr Cooper.

'Here,' said Paula.

'Sophie Johnston.'

'Here.'

'Trevor King.'

'Here.'

'Josephine Lewis.'

Silence. Everyone looked around.

'Josephine Lewis,' Mr Cooper repeated.

'Oh, that'll be me,' came a voice. It was the new girl. 'No-one ever calls me Josephine,' she said.

'What do they call you?' asked Mr Cooper.

'Jordy,' she said. At least that's what it sounded like.

'Jordy?' said Mr Cooper.

'No, Jordy!' said the girl.

'Perhaps you'd like to come and write it on the board,' said Mr Cooper.

Sam felt his heart begin to pound. If *he'd* been in her shoes – in a new class and singled out – he'd have felt awful. But the new girl seemed unconcerned. She strode up to the white-board confidently, took a pen and wrote her name. 'J-o-d-i-e.'

'Jodie!' said Mr Cooper.

'That's what I said,' said the girl.

'It's your accent,' said Mr Cooper. 'Yorkshire, is it?'

The girl grinned. 'Born and bred,' she said.

Sam watched her with a mixture of admiration and amazement. She was *so* confident. For a start, she had skin that Sam would have given anything for. It was the type which never blushed. And then there were the eyes. Large and green, they stared up into Mr Cooper's face without any trace of shyness as she spoke.

'I don't mind what folk call me – apart from Josephine!'

Everyone laughed. Sam looked at the letters on the board. Jodie.

No, he thought. For him at least, the new girl would always be Jordy.

CHAPTER TEN

In the darkness underground, Tom Tiddler was resting. The previous night's digging had exhausted him, and he was still tired. The smell was gone and, as he gathered strength for the coming night, Tom Tiddler's sleep was peaceful and undisturbed.

Now that the memory of Tom Tiddler has returned to this world in bodily form, what should we call him? Imp? Fairy? Hobgoblin? Troll? Perhaps it does not matter. Only one thing is certain. No-one comes back from beyond without a very good reason.

Perhaps the question ought to be this. Has Tom Tiddler returned for good or evil?

CHAPTER ELEVEN

By dinner-time, Sam was starving. Six weeks of
his mum's Bean-Bake and Lentil Surprise had
left him looking forward to school dinners. He
loaded up his tray with beefburgers, double
chips and beans, apricot crumble and ice cream,
a carton of milk and an apple.

The hall was practically empty by the time he
had finally finished eating. Sam stood up, patted
his stomach contentedly, burped – and made his
way to the playground. As he stepped outside, he
stopped dead in his tracks. Sam could not believe
his eyes.

Under Jordy's guidance, the whole of class 8C
was in the middle of some game or other. Even
Maurice Davies, who would normally have

disappeared into the library. Even Elaine Pritchard, who would normally be filing her nails. Even Craig Martin! What was more, they weren't just playing, they were *enjoying* playing!

Sam was impressed. Who was this person who could transform thirty bored, gum-chewing twelve-year-olds into what looked like a class of enthusiastic primary school kids?

In the middle of the circle, chalked on the tarmac, stood Craig. He was *The Vampire*. An odd choice, Sam thought, given the state of his teeth. Stun them with bad breath and then gum them to un-death! he thought with a smirk.

Then again, he could understand why Jordy had picked him as the bogeyman. Teeth or no teeth, Craig made an excellent Vampire. As he flapped menacingly from one edge of the circle to the other in pursuit of his victims, the air became charged with nervous excitement.

The rules of the game were simple. The boys and girls stood around the circle waiting for a moment when the Vampire was otherwise engaged, to run in and 'steal' one of his *blood-red rubies* – one of the stones which had been scattered around the circle – without being caught. Those who *were* captured had to remain in the circle until released by someone who would break the Vampire's spell by crawling between their legs. They also had to forfeit a ruby.

The aim, of course, was to outwit the Vampire,

and the winner was the first to steal five rubies. Anyone who ran out of rubies was out of the game.

As Sam watched, he realized how clever the rules were. Although it was perilous to release someone who had been captured, it was essential. The more people there were on the outside of the circle, the more the Vampire had to contend with. To stand *any* chance of stealing five rubies, everyone had to work together.

Sam looked at Jordy. At that moment, she turned her head.

'Come on!' she mouthed at him.

Sam nodded. The next minute, he was standing next to the others, on the edge of the circle. Already, he had been caught up in the general tension of the game. Yet, as the excited squealing and screams of horror continued, Sam began to feel uneasy. There was something a little too familiar about the way the children were dashing in and out of the chalked circle. And what was that they were shouting out? Sam realized he was beginning to shiver.

'How many have you got?' asked a voice.

Sam turned. It was Waz. 'None yet,' he said.

'Go on, then,' he said. 'The Vampire's up the other end. Go in and get one!'

'What is it I have to yell out?' he said.

'Here I am in the Vampire's lair,
Picking up blood-red rubies!'
said Waz. 'Go on. Now!'

With his heart in his mouth, Sam ran into the circle. He picked up a stone, straightened up, and looked around giddily. His head was swimming. His ears were echoing.

'The words!' Waz called out.

Oh yes, thought Sam. The words. 'Here I am . . .' he shouted. 'Here I am . . . Here I am . . .'

'. . . in the Vampire's lair,' Waz shouted urgently. 'Get on with it!'

But Sam did not hear his friend's words. The nightmare had been broken and he knew exactly what he had to say. Loud and clear, he cried out:

'Here I am in Tom Tiddler's Ground,
Picking up gold and silver!'

CHAPTER TWELVE

That first afternoon back at school couldn't have gone more slowly for Sam. He didn't like science at the best of times, and with so many other things on his mind, the double period seemed to last for ever.

When the bell did finally go, Sam was up and out before it had even stopped ringing. He ran down the stairs, two at a time and skidded round into the corridor.

'Don't run, Dillon!' came the familiar voice of Mr Barnes the headmaster.

'Sorry, sir,' said Sam, slowing down to an awkward, exaggerated walk.

In the boys' cloakroom at last, Sam grabbed

his coat and slipped out again, before the end-of-school stampede got going.

As he strode across the playground towards the school gates, he heard someone calling him. At first, Sam pretended he hadn't noticed. He just wanted to get home. But the voice was insistent.

'Sa-am!' it shouted impatiently. 'Sam!'

Sam turned round, and there – standing next to the main door – was Jordy. She smiled and ran over to him.

'Hiya!' she said, as she caught up with him. 'I wanted to ask you something.'

'Yeah!' said Sam. 'What?'

'Nothing, if you're going to be like that!' Jordy snapped.

Sam stared back in surprise. The new girl was nothing if not direct. 'Sorry,' he said. 'I've got . . . a lot on my mind.'

Jordy raised her eyebrows, but said nothing. They walked down the road in silence. Finally, it was Sam who spoke.

'So what was that question?' he said.

'Oh, it doesn't matter,' said Jordy.

'Come on,' Sam said.

'Well,' she said slowly. 'It was about the Vampire game . . .' The back of Sam's neck began to tingle ominously. 'What did you think of it, by the way?' she asked.

47

'The Vampire game . . .' Sam repeated. He needed time to work out exactly what he wanted to say. If he blabbed all about the nightmare and Tom Tiddler, he was sure that Jordy would think he was some kind of loony. 'It was fun,' he said finally.

'Yes, *I* thought so,' said Jordy. 'Grandmother will be pleased . . . Of course, it's an old game,' she went on. 'It doesn't have to be a Vampire.'

'No?' said Sam.

'No. It just needs some kind of a bogeyman. Sometimes a historical figure; sometimes someone local,' she explained. 'In Shropshire he's called "Boney" – short for Bonaparte. You know, Napoleon Bonaparte. So the game must be at least two hundred years old. In Yorkshire, he's called Tom Tinker. And in Derbyshire, Tommy Tinder. Tinkers, gypsies, charcoal-makers; they were all treated with suspicion . . .'

Sam laughed. 'How come you know so much about it?' he said.

'Oh, it's Grandmother,' said Jordy. 'She's writing a book about all the games children used to play.'

'Writing a book!' said Sam, impressed. He thought of his own gran. More of the knitting, baking variety, Sam's gran never wrote anything, apart from the occasional Christmas or birthday card. And even then she wrote in capital letters!

'She likes me to try out the games she finds,' Jordy was saying. 'Grandmother calls me her field researcher! It's how I earn my weekly allowance,' she added.

Weekly allowance, thought Sam wistfully. These days he was lucky if he got any pocket money at all. He sighed. Jordy stopped dead in her tracks, turned and eyed Sam closely.

'Am I boring you?' she said.

'No,' said Sam, genuinely shocked. 'No. Not at all . . .'

'I know I can go on a bit . . .' she said.

'No. Honest,' said Sam. 'It's interesting.'

'Where was I, then?' she said.

'Weekly allowance,' said Sam.

'Before that.'

'Boney – and Tom Tinker,' said Sam, and as he did so, he had the most curious feeling of *déjà vu* – he was *sure* he'd done this before. Walking along with Jordy, talking about the game, stopping opposite the statue on the roundabout . . . Suddenly he knew exactly what she was going to say next. His heart pounded. His head itched.

'Of course,' Jordy was saying, 'taking the country as a whole, the most common name for the bogeyman is . . .'

Sam wiped away the sweat on his brow with his sleeve.

'Tom Tiddler.'

Sam shuddered. It was as though the sweat

49

had suddenly been turned to ice.

'Here we are in Tom Tiddler's Ground . . .'

'Picking up gold and silver,' said Sam quietly.

'You *did* know it!' she exclaimed. 'I thought I heard you in the playground . . . Have you played it before?'

Sam felt his face turning red. 'No,' he said. 'I mean . . . I must have heard it somewhere,' he said, vaguely. His nightmare was, on no account, to be mentioned!

'Oh, Grandmother will definitely want to see you!' Jordy exclaimed. 'It's so unusual to find kids who know the old games. She'll want to know everything! It's a shame she won't be there today.' She paused, and then – pointing down Parkside Avenue – added, 'I live over there.'

'Near the rec.,' said Sam.

'St George's?' said Jordy. 'Directly opposite.'

'Must be nice,' he said, enviously.

'It is,' said Jordy. 'Shame it's only temporary.'

'Temporary?' Sam repeated.

Jordy sighed. 'As soon as Grandmother's completed her research here, we're going up to Scotland.'

'Oh,' said Sam. 'So you won't be staying,' he said.

'Till Christmas,' said Jordy. 'Maybe Easter. It depends how it goes. Anyway, I'll be here tomorrow. I'll see you then, OK?' she said.

Sam nodded. 'Yeah. See you,' he said.

50

As Sam made his way down the High Street, his head was spinning. What a day! Not only had he remembered a part of his nightmare for the first time ever, but he'd met someone who might be able to help him understand it. The game, the rhyme . . . Tom Tiddler . . .

Suddenly, Sam gasped. Going over the nightmare in his head, the most terrifying part of all had come back to him. The hand! How could he have forgotten? There had been a hand reaching from the earth. It had grabbed him and spun him round and round . . .

Sam trembled. His mouth tasted metallic. He had wanted so much to remember the nightmare when he was awake. Now, he wondered whether he hadn't made a dreadful mistake. If having the dream at night was bad, then remembering it during the day, too, was surely going to be twice as unpleasant.

CHAPTER THIRTEEN

As the days turned into weeks, Sam spent every night in a deep, dreamless – or rather *nightmareless* – sleep. Perhaps it was, as he himself had thought, that by remembering the dream, he had been released from it.

Whatever, the terror had faded. Now, it was just a memory, little stronger than the memory of a particularly gruesome horror film. Still there, but somehow detached – which was exactly how he would describe Jordy Lewis.

She was friendly enough, but then she was friendly to everyone. Danno, Waz, Elaine, Craig . . . everyone! And as for meeting Jordy's grandmother, well, she'd obviously forgotten all about it. Sam decided to do likewise.

Apart from this one little disappointment, things were going OK for Sam. School was easy. Craig Martin had stopped nicking his chocolate – Danno had threatened to kick his head in if he caught him at it again! Even life at home had improved. His dad was working hard, and his mum had taken a part-time evening job in the local off-licence.

'We've turned the corner,' his dad said one morning. He'd worked all through the night, and was having breakfast with Sam before heading for bed. He cuffed his son playfully on the cheek. 'We're on the up, Sam.'

Sam grinned. When his dad was feeling good, he was the nicest man in the world.

'And to prove it,' announced his mum, 'a new winter jacket!'

Sam turned and stared.

'Where did you get that?' asked his dad.

'Down the High Street,' said his mum vaguely.

'The charity shop,' said Sam.

'They've some very good stuff in there,' said his mum defensively. 'Some of it's hardly been worn.'

Sam continued to stare at the jacket.

'Let's have a look,' said Sam's dad. He peered inside the collar. 'It's a good make,' he said. 'Looks almost new. Hang on . . . There's a name here.'

'Oh, I'll get it out with some nail varnish

remover,' she said, grabbing at the jacket.

But his dad held tight. 'Ted . . .' he said, squinting at the faint letters. 'Ted Barker.'

'Ted Barker!' Sam exclaimed.

'Name sounds familiar,' said his dad. 'Do I know him?'

'He's that old man down the road,' said Sam. 'Always up on his allotment.'

'What? The one who . . .'

'. . . Died. Yes,' said Sam. 'In the middle of his Brussels sprouts. Probably wearing *that*!' he said, pointing at the jacket. 'I am *not* wearing it.'

'It's a perfectly good jacket,' said his mum.

'Yeah, but you can see his point, Sal,' said his dad.

Thank you, Dad! Thank you!

'It's bucketing down outside!' said his mum.

'I'll wear my old one,' said Sam.

'You can't,' his mum snapped.

'It's not *that* bad,' said Sam.

She folded her arms. 'I got the new one on part exchange.'

'Oh, MU-UM!' Sam shouted. 'Well, I'm not wearing it. I'm not! And you can't make me!'

'You will do as you are told, young man,' his mum shouted back. 'If I say wear the jacket, then you will wear the jacket.'

'If I do, it's going in the first bin I come to,' Sam said defiantly.

'Sam!' his dad said firmly. And Sam knew he'd

gone too far. Not that he wasn't prepared to go farther! As far as was necessary. Sam – unlike Ted Barker – wouldn't be seen dead in the jacket, and that was that. 'It can be exchanged, I take it,' said his dad.

Sam kept looking down at the table. Come on, Dad, he urged silently.

'In that case,' he said, 'I suggest the pair of you go in tomorrow and find something that he *will* wear.'

Sam felt his mum's eyes boring into the top of his head.

'In the meantime,' he continued, 'since it's raining, I'll take Sam to school in the car. All right?'

Sam looked up. His mum was nodding. He should have felt happy but now that he'd won, Sam felt guilty. She looked so miserable.

'Go on, then, the pair of you,' she said.

It wasn't until they were driving along that Sam spoke. The rain was hammering down on the roof of the car.

'I'm sorry I shouted,' he said.

'I'm not the one you need to say sorry to, am I?' said his dad.

'No,' said Sam, softly. 'Thanks for the lift, anyway.'

'That's all right, son,' said his dad. He snorted with amusement. 'And to tell you the truth, I can understand you being a bit squeamish.'

Sam nodded. If his dad wanted to think Sam was uneasy about the jacket because of its recent history, then so be it. But he was wrong!

Sam didn't have anything against second-hand clothes – after all, his pride and joy was an original 1939 'Phillies' baseball shirt. Nor did he particularly mind that someone had probably died in the jacket. Nor even that that someone was 'Batty' Ted Barker – he could easily have gone over the name with felt tip. No. The thing Sam had against the jacket was the jacket itself.

It was an anorak! A *long* anorak! A long, *green* anorak! A long, green, *padded, nylon* anorak! A swot anorak! A dork anorak! A Maurice Davies anorak! And there was no way on earth that Sam Dillon was ever *ever* going to turn up at school looking like Maurice Davies.

'What the . . !' Sam's dad suddenly exclaimed, and slammed on his brakes.

Sam braced himself for the sudden jolt – but it never came. They weren't slowing down at all. Sam realized they were aquaplaning out of control.

Pete Dillon yanked desperately at the wheel – now this way, now that, all the while pumping away at the brakes. But the steering wheel refused to steer, the tyres refused to grip, and the car refused to stop. Instead, it began to spin round to the right – into the oncoming traffic.

The bus driver coming the other way had

witnessed it all. He'd seen the dog running out in front of the taxi. He'd watched the driver lose control. He'd managed to stop his bus, but now could only look on helplessly as the car rammed into his front, jumped up the kerb and ended up folded around a lamppost.

Sam opened his eyes. His dad, still gripping the steering wheel, was simply staring ahead of him.

'Are you all right?' asked Sam.

'It's a complete write-off,' said his dad quietly. 'I don't believe it.' His face was white with rage. 'If I ever get my hands on that dog . . . If I ever get my hands on its *owner* . . . I'll . . . I'll . . .' He turned on Sam. 'If you hadn't made such a fuss about that damned coat, none of this would have happened.'

Sam looked away. He wanted to cry. He wanted to hit his dad – to punch that ugly, angry, accusing face. More than both of these, he wanted a hug.

Sam's dad, however, was clearly in no mood for hugs. 'I don't know what you're just sitting there for,' he snapped. 'We're not going anywhere.'

Sam nodded. He pulled the handle and pushed on the door. The car filled with the sound of metal scraping on metal. Sam climbed out. 'I'll see you later, then,' he said.

If his dad made a reply, Sam didn't hear it.

Sighing miserably, he pulled his blazer collar up and set off into the torrential rain. He could only hope that by the time he got home, things would have sorted themselves out somehow.

The day went quickly. Too quickly. Before he knew it, Sam was home again. As he closed the front door quietly behind him, it was instantly clear his hopes had been in vain.

In fact, as he listened to his mum and dad talking from the hallway, Sam realized that things were even worse than he'd thought. That morning, the supermarket gossip had become reality. All the part-timers had been laid off.

'I just don't know how we're going to survive,' he heard his mum sobbing. 'What are we going to *do*?'

CHAPTER FOURTEEN

Sam went to bed early that Friday night. His mum had gone to the off-licence at six, leaving him alone with his dad. As usual, they watched telly together, but the atmosphere was awful – Sam's dad sat there stony-faced through a succession of sitcoms, and when the news came on and he learnt that Eric Crisp had been sold to United for a record eleven million pounds, he exploded with fury.

'Eleven million!' he exclaimed. 'It's obscene! It's appalling! It's disgraceful! It's . . .'

Sam didn't wait to hear what else it was. He slipped out of the sitting room, went up to his bedroom and lay on the bed, thinking what *he* could do with eleven million pounds.

This time, when he dropped off to sleep, there was no pleasant introduction to the nightmare. No game of cricket. No ice-cream van.

Sam found himself standing in the middle of the dark forest, quite alone. He listened, but there was not a sound. No birdsong. No wind. Even the nightmarish sound of the children's squealing voices was absent this time.

Swirling round his legs was a thick fog, which was coiling up out of the ground like a mass of pea-green snakes. Higher and higher it writhed, twisting itself around Sam's body. Sam gasped, but as he did so, the fog crept into his mouth and up his nose. He tasted metal. He smelt sulphur. It wormed its way into his ears, muffling the silence. It filled his eyes with a curious, pale green blindness.

'It can't do you any harm,' said Sam, trying to reassure himself. 'It's only fog.'

But it was the thickest fog Sam had ever known. Unable to see, Sam had no idea which direction to take. He knew only that he must not stand still.

The leaves of the bushes and brambles were black with grime and, as Sam trudged through the dense undergrowth, his hands, his face, his clothes, were soon covered in the oily soot. Not that Sam noticed. Neither did he notice the thorns tearing at his uniform. On and on he went, deeper into the forest, unaware that – with every step – he was being transformed from schoolboy to street urchin.

'How much further?' he complained.

As if in response, the trees seemed to part and, as Sam stepped forward, he found himself in the circular clearing once again. With his heart racing and his stomach churning, he peered into the gloom.

All around him, he heard the sound of sharp intakes of breath. Sam stopped.

'It's too dangerous,' he whispered to himself. 'If only I could see.'

No sooner had the words left his mouth, than Sam found he could see – and instantly wished he could not. It all happened so fast.

As the fog thinned, Sam saw a dark shape in front of him; a shape which – as the fog dissolved completely – revealed itself as a small, hunched creature in dirty rags. It was standing with its back to him.

Sam stared in horror at the lowered head, terrified that the creature would look round. Scarcely daring to breathe, he began to back away. He hadn't gone more than two steps when he heard a sudden BANG! echoing around the forest. The creature raised its head.

All at once, the clearing echoed with the sound of screaming. The boys and girls around the circle who had seen the creature's face screeched in terror, and ran off as fast as they could. Not wanting to be left, the others joined them. Within seconds, only Sam was left.

Alone. Frozen to the spot. Why couldn't *he* move? Why wouldn't his legs take *him* away before it was too late?

Imperceptibly, at first, the creature began to turn. Sam felt the blood pounding in his temples. 'Run!' his brain commanded; but still his legs would not obey. A gnarled profile came into view, and Sam gasped as a black and yellow eye peered back at him.

Suddenly, the creature spun right around. Sam found himself face to face with the most hideous, the most gruesome, the most fearsome . . . *thing* he had ever seen in his life.

It was short – shorter than Sam. Its legs were twisted, its spine was bent, and the hump on its back pushed the head over to one side. Long, matted hair and a thick beard had swallowed up most of its face. All Sam could see was the eyes, loose in their sockets, and a warty, potato-shaped lump that was its nose.

'NO!' Sam screamed. 'NOOOOOOO!'

He closed his eyes. He opened them again. The monster was still there. Worse! As Sam stood there, unable to turn away, the beard split open to reveal a deep dark hole, lined with stubby black teeth.

In a cracked, high-pitched voice, the creature

began to speak. And as it spoke, it advanced towards the boy.

'See how it is, and not how it seems.
The Tiddler you see is the Tom of bad
        dreams.'

The creature got closer and closer and closer – and *still* Sam could not move. The words continued; bewildering, hypnotic.

'See not how it seems, but see how it is,'

The creature stopped walking. Standing directly in front of Sam, it fixed the boy with an unblinking stare and reached inside its tattered jacket.

'And help yourself to all that is his!'

As the verse came to an end, the creature made a sudden movement. The hand re-appeared. Something metal glinted in the acid-lemon light.

'A knife!' Sam gasped.

The creature lunged out – but Sam was too quick for it. He jumped back. He turned. He ran. At last, his body was again taking orders from his brain again; at last, he had managed to break free.

And yet, no matter how far he ran, Sam could still hear Tom Tiddler's voice echoing through the trees.

'See how it is!' it said, over and over.

CHAPTER FIFTEEN

Sam woke up with a start. He looked around his bedroom. It was morning – thank Heavens! Though, once again, the nightmare remained with him. And this time, not just in snippets.

'*See how it is*,' said Sam slowly. '*Not how it seems. I* can *remember it. How did the rest go? The tiddler here . . . is the Tom of bad dreams.* I can remember it all!'

Excited, Sam grabbed a pen and began scribbling the words down on a pad of paper. About the fog, the sooty leaves, the clearing, the concentric rings . . .

And then, he wrote, *I saw this horrible creature. Tom Tiddler himself! Not just a hand, but the whole person – if it WAS a person.*

With the memory of the fearful little monster still fresh in his mind, Sam drew it as best he could. The thick hair, the staring eyes, the stumpy teeth . . . 'Like Craig's,' he muttered. The humped back and bandy legs; the tattered clothes.

He was busy shading in the warts on the bulbous nose when Sam heard that he wasn't the only one awake in the house. His parents were at it *again*!

'What do you mean "an accident"?' his mum yelled.

'I didn't *mean* to do it,' his dad shouted back. He sounded like a defiant little boy.

It *was* an accident, thought Sam. What with the dog and the torrential rain, his dad had never stood a chance. And yet, as the shouting continued, Sam began to suspect that they weren't talking about the car at all. He listened carefully.

'It just slipped out of my hand,' said his dad.

'Slipped!' said his mum. 'You mean you threw it.'

'I was angry!' his dad shouted.

'You're always angry!' his mum shouted back.

'Well, what do you expect?' he said. 'I'm in debt up to my eyeballs. I've lost my job, I've wrecked my taxi, I've—'

'Smashed the telly,' his mum yelled.

'It was already broken,' his dad protested.

'Oh, stop lying!'

'It was, I tell you! Ten-twenty, it was. I was watching the news and suddenly the picture just went. Then . . . I didn't notice at first . . . But the volume went. Honest, Sal, there were sparks and flashes on the screen and this crackling whistle, getting louder and louder. I thought the whole lot was going to blow up—'

'So you decided to do the job yourself!'

'The remote was slippery,' said Sam's dad. 'It was the fish and chips.'

'Now I've heard everything!' stormed his mum. There was a long pause. Then his mum spoke again, more quietly now. Sam strained to hear. 'Anyway,' she was saying, 'there wasn't anything wrong with the telly. The postman was saying. It was that interference again. Only stronger . . .'

Sam sucked his pencil. So the interference had struck again! He remembered, only too well, the last time it had happened. His *first* encounter with Tom Tiddler. Now it had happened again. Could it really be just a coincidence?

At that moment, the phone rang. Sam heard his mum answering.

'Sam,' she called up the stairs. 'It's for you.'

Sam leapt off the bed, raced downstairs and picked up the receiver. 'Hello?' he said.

It was Waz. He and the others were meeting

up at the rec. for a game of footie. Did he fancy joining them? Did he ever!

'Mum,' Sam called. 'Is it OK if—'

'Yes, yes. Anything,' came the weary reply. 'Just make sure you're back by one.'

'I'll see you in ten minutes,' said Sam to Waz.

Back upstairs again, Sam quickly got washed and dressed. He was just about to go when he noticed the pencil and paper on his bed. The nightmare came back to him.

'Might as well get it all down,' he said to himself. 'Before I forget.'

Then, while he was reciting the words, wrote Sam, *he put his hand in his pocket . . . 'And help yourself to all that is his!' he said. And then out comes his hand again – quick as a flash – with a knife in it. That's when I ran. And ran and ran, until I woke up.*

Sam read the whole lot through. Why was he bothering? he wondered. What was the point in writing it all down? It was just a nightmare. That's all!

Yet, Sam remained unconvinced that it *was* just a nightmare. Icy shivers ran up and down his neck. It was as if someone – or something – was deliberately trying to communicate with him.

CHAPTER SIXTEEN

Sam decided to take the notes about the nightmare with him. He didn't want his mum to read about it. She would only worry. Not that his mum was a snooper. But she *did* clean very thoroughly! Sam had asked her not to once, but she'd misunderstood him.

'Oh, I don't mind doing it,' she said. 'It's no trouble.'

'But . . . I lose things when you tidy up,' he said.

'Sam!' his mum said. 'You're blushing! Are you telling me you've got secrets you want to keep from your old mum?'

Sam cringed at the memory. Yes, he thought. I have. He tore the piece of paper from the pad, folded it three times and slipped it into the back pocket of his jeans. 'And I can wipe my own bottom now, as well!' he muttered angrily.

Trainers on, Sam left his room and crept along the bare boards of the landing – carpets were something else which had been put on *temporary hold* when Pete Dillon lost his job.

Halfway down the stairs, Sam stopped and peered in through the sitting-room door. There was the television; screen shattered. Beside it lay the remote.

Oh, Dad! Sam thought.

He continued down the stairs and slipped out of the front door without making a sound. He'd told Waz ten minutes. Finishing off the account of the nightmare had taken more than that. If his mum insisted on him having breakfast, too, then they'd start the game without him.

I can always grab something later, he thought.

How *much* later this would be, Sam did not yet know. By the time he did finally get something to eat, however, he was extremely hungry indeed.

Waz, Danno, Gopher and half a dozen others were already kicking the ball around when Sam got to the park. His arrival meant that they could now play five-a-side.

'Watch'er,' he said.

'You're late,' said Waz.

'It was me dad,' said Sam – which wasn't exactly true; but then, since his parents blamed him for everything that happened to *them*. . .

'How come?' said Waz.

'You're not going to believe this,' said Sam. 'He only smashed the telly! Chucked the remote through the screen—'

'You're kidding,' said Waz. 'Our telly *blew up* last night.'

'What time?' Sam asked nervously.

'Bout half-ten,' he said. 'The late film was about to come on, and . . .'

Sam was no longer listening. About half past ten! Perhaps his dad hadn't smashed the telly after all. But if that was the case, then what exactly had made it – them – explode? Suddenly Sam felt very scared. If there *was* a connection between the nightmare and the interference, then . . . Then, perhaps he—

'Get a grip!' Sam muttered to himself. 'Dreams do not make tellies or anything else explode. And that's that!'

CHAPTER SEVENTEEN

Back under the ground once more, in the comforting safety of darkness, Tom Tiddler was dreaming. He was dreaming of completing the task for which he had returned to earth. As he dreamt, he paid attention, for Tom Tiddler understood the power of dreams.

He knew that dreams could shape a life; he knew that dreams could change the world. He also knew that those changes need not always be for the better – that the dreams of the few could become the nightmare for everybody else.

Troubled for an instant, Tom Tiddler grumbled and rolled over in his sleep.

'But you,' he mumbled drowsily, dreamfully, 'you will get what's coming to you. Mark . . . my . . . words.'

CHAPTER EIGHTEEN

Sam had just taken over from Gopher in goal, when the dog appeared. Ignoring the game of football in progress, it trotted diagonally across the pitch.

'Oy!' yelled Waz.

The dog, a medium-sized mongrel, took no notice. With its long, thick, reddish coat, it looked as if one of its parents was a setter. And if that was the case, then the other had to be a spaniel. Its ears looked like a couple of furry flannels that had been stuck on as an afterthought.

'Get out of it,' shouted Danno, running at the animal in a dummy charge.

The dog neither looked round nor speeded up.

Instead, cool as you like – while the boys watched in horrified disbelief – it crouched, it strained, it did its business. Then, pausing only for the briefest of inspections, it continued on its way.

'You dirty little . . .' Danno shouted, as he rushed after the dog.

Gopher joined him. 'Wait till I get my hands on you!' he yelled.

Hearing their angry voices at last, the dog took fright and dashed off to the far end of the playing field. Sam ran out of the goal to try and head it off. But the dog was too fast for him. It dummied to the left, dodged to the right and, as Sam fell to the ground, raced past him into the woods.

With its long hair flat against its body, and its ears pinned back by the wind, the dog looked quite different. Smaller. Sleeker. Sam knew he had seen it before. 'The accident!' he exclaimed.

Certainly the dog looked redder now, but then it was chucking it down that morning and it had been soaked to the skin. No. Sam was sure. The dog which had interrupted their game so disgustingly, was the same dog that had made his dad crash. He turned round. 'That dog—' he said.

'Yeah,' said Waz. 'I wish I'd caught hold of it!'

'Gonna wring its neck, were you?' Danno jeered.

'No,' said Waz, and smirked. 'I was going to wait for its owner to turn up. And then I'd have wrung *his* neck!'

'Or *her* neck?' said Danno, and shrugged towards the figure coming across the park.

Sam looked round. 'Oh, no!' he groaned.

'Rapper!' shouted the girl as she came closer. 'RAPPER!' She came right up to the boys. 'Oh, it's you lot,' she said.

'Hello, Jordy,' they said.

'I don't suppose you've seen my dog, have you?' she said.

'Middle-sized mongrel?' said Danno.

Jordy nodded. 'A setter/spaniel cross,' she said.

'Long red hair?' said Gopher. 'Floppy ears.'

'You *have* seen him!' said Jordy.

The boys nodded as one.

'We've seen him, all right,' said Gopher.

'Yeah,' said Waz. 'We've seen Crapper, all right.'

'His name's Rapper,' said Jordy sharply.

'Well, it shouldn't be,' Waz retorted. 'Look!' He pointed to the coil of dog mess. It was still steaming.

Sam knew that at this point, if he was her, he would have turned bright red with embarrassment. But Sam was not Jordy Lewis; and Jordy was certainly not Sam Dillon. With her sallow, unchanging complexion it was impossible to tell what she was feeling. When she spoke, however, Sam guessed that embarrassment was the last thing on her mind.

'I hope you haven't hurt him,' she said, glaring round.

'Course we haven't,' said Danno sheepishly.

'But you frightened him, eh?' she said. 'Ten of you against one of him. Very brave!' She looked around the park. 'So which way did he go?' she said.

'Into the woods, I think,' said Danno.

'Into the woods,' Jordy repeated flatly. 'I'm not allowed in the woods on my own.'

'None of us are,' said Gopher.

'But if that's where he's gone,' Jordy sighed, 'then that's where I shall have to go . . .'

'I'll come with you,' said Sam.

Jordy turned to him. 'Would you?' she said.

Sam nodded.

Ignoring the 'woooaarrh!' noises that Waz was making, Sam and Jordy headed for the wood.

'What about our five-a-side?' Danno called out.

'Play *three*-a-side!' Jordy shouted over her shoulder.

'What?' they all shouted back.

'Think about it,' said Jordy.

CHAPTER NINETEEN

'So,' said Sam. He and Jordy had been walking through the wood for several minutes in silence. Sam was beginning to feel awkward. 'So,' he repeated, 'how do you like it *down south*?'

Jordy snorted. 'I'm getting on better than Rapper,' she said. 'Poor thing's been a bag of nerves ever since we moved.'

'Why do you let him out, then?' said Sam.

'We *don't* let him out,' Jordy snapped. 'He keeps escaping. Jumping out of windows; breaking the fence down ... He's desperate to get back to our old house. Or to get away from here, at any rate.' Sam listened carefully. 'I don't know what it is,' she went on. 'But *something* is upsetting him. Last night! He wouldn't stop howling! I hardly slept a wink.'

Sam nodded. The back of his neck was tingling.

'And then this morning! When he did finally stop howling, he went berserk. Racing round the house, he was . . . In the end, he squeezed himself through the cat flap. God knows how! And he was away again.'

Sam realized his imagination was beginning to get the better of him again. Radio interference, exploding tellies – and now mad dogs! And all on the nights when he had the nightmare.

'And school?' he said, desperate for a change of subject.

'School?' said Jordy. 'It's all right. Except for the Clever Dicks taking the rise out of my accent. It's "grass" and "path" – not gr-aaaah-ss and p-aaaaah-th,' she said. 'You say fat. You say ass. You don't say f-aaaah-t aaaah-ss.'

Sam laughed. 'You can do!' he said.

Realizing what she'd said, Jordy laughed, too. 'I'll tell you what,' she said. 'Of all the people I've met down here, I like you best.'

Sam's mouth twisted itself into an embarrassed grin. He wanted to say, 'I like you, too'. But these were not the words he uttered. What he actually said was, 'But why?'

'Fishing for compliments, eh?' said Jordy.

'No, I—' Sam said.

'Because you're sweet,' she said.

Sam winced. Not 'sweet'. Anything but 'sweet'!

'You're thoughtful. You're sensitive. You're honest . . .'

But was he, though? Sam wondered. If he was honest, he'd have told Jordy that it was her dog that caused his dad's accident. 'Can you be considerate *and* honest?' he wondered.

Jordy laughed. 'But the best thing about you,' she said, 'is you're weird!'

'*Me* weird?' Sam laughed. 'How the heck *do* you play three-a-side football?'

'With nine players?' said Jordy, serious again. 'Easy. Three teams of three, right? Three goals – in a triangle. Three goalies. Six attackers/defenders – two per team. Right?'

Sam nodded.

'Each team can score in *either* of the other teams' goals.'

'And scoring?' said Sam.

'Depends whether you want to concentrate on attacking or defending,' said Jordy. 'Either each team can count the total number of goals it scores. Or the goalies can count the number of goals they let in. Or both – but you'd probably need a pen and paper!'

Sam nodded. The more he thought about it,

the cleverer the game seemed. Faster than five-a-side – and much more skilful! Passing would have to be spot-on, and each player would need to be good both at attack and defence.

'And you thought this up yourself?' said Sam.

Jordy nodded. 'Best is with three teams of four.'

'Has it got a name?' said Sam.

'No,' said Jordy. 'I haven't—'

'How about Triball?' said Sam.

'Maybe,' said Jordy. 'And if we ever had a knockout competition we could call it Triball Warfare!'

Sam laughed. 'And if—'

'Shh!' Jordy hissed, and stopped walking.

'What is it?' said Sam.

'Sssshh!' Jordy hissed more insistently.

Sam listened.

'Did you hear that?' Jordy whispered.

'No,' said Sam, shaking his head.

'There,' said Jordy.

This time Sam heard it, too. It was the sound of a dog in pain; yelping, whining.

'Rapper!' Jordy yelled, and tore off into the undergrowth.

'Wait for me,' shouted Sam, as he rushed after her. He had no intention of being left on his own. 'Wait for me!'

CHAPTER TWENTY

Sam's heart was pounding as they ran deeper and deeper into the trees. What had made the dog cry out? What was now making it howl so heart-rendingly?

'That's how he sounded last night,' Jordy panted. 'I don't like it.'

'Neither do I!' said Sam quietly.

On and on they ran. Tripped by roots and scratched by brambles, the pair of them kept on in the direction of the howling.

'I think he's over there somewhere,' said Jordy, darting off to the left.

Sam made sure he kept right behind her. The next moment, they emerged into the clearing.

Sam gasped. 'It can't be,' he muttered, as he gazed round at the brown ring, the grey ring, the black inner circle . . . 'It isn't possible.'

But it could. And it was. Sam was back in his nightmare. Only this time, he was awake.

'RAPPER!' Jordy exclaimed, and raced towards the dog, cowering by the edge of the clearing. She flung her arms around his neck. 'Rapper, boy. What *happened*?'

'Is he all right?' Sam asked.

But Jordy didn't answer. She was too busy scratching Rapper's stomach as he rolled about on his back, seemingly none the worse for his experience. 'So what was all that howling about?' she said. 'Eh? Eh? Eh?'

Sam turned away and walked to the centre of the circle. He kicked at the black soil. It was sooty. Burnt. He shook his head. 'What *did* happen here?' he wondered. 'How did . . .'

Suddenly, Sam knew that something was wrong. The atmosphere had changed. The air had become thick, like treacly glass. Sam could hardly move – and when he tried to call out, his words were gravelly, low and so, so slow.

'Jooor . . . Deeayyy . . .' he moaned.

What was more – and just as Sam had feared – Jordy was unable to hear his cries. In awful slow-motion, she continued to pat, scratch and tickle Rapper, unaware that anything might be wrong.

You don't have to be on your own to be alone, Sam realized.

The next moment he felt a warm, sickly wind blowing around his head. His mouth tasted of dirty metal. He heard a scratching sound, spun around – and there was the hideous dwarf once again.

Tom Tiddler grinned his toothless grin. He seemed to be enjoying Sam's fear and discomfort. He licked his cracked lips with his slug-like tongue, and started to speak.

'One is dead, but not forgotten,
A name lived on when the body was
   rotten.'

Horrified, Sam clamped his hands tightly to his ears. 'I don't want to hear,' he said. 'I don't want to know.'

But Tom Tiddler would not be silenced.

'One is forgotten, but is not dead,' he
   continued.

'Stop it!' Sam cried, backing away. 'Leave me alone.'

'Which Tom Tiddler is in your head?' he
   roared.

84

With that, the little man lunged forward, arm outstretched, with his index and middle fingers aimed at Sam's face.

Terrified that he was about to be blinded, Sam tried to duck, to turn away – but in vain. The treacly air wouldn't let him. He shut his eyes and waited for the inevitable.

The next instant, the fingers made contact. Sam screamed.

But the nails did not gouge out his eyes. They did not even scratch him. Instead, Sam felt the cold, scaly skin of Tom Tiddler's fingertips pressing gently – yes, gently – against his eyeballs. He was overcome with the feeling of falling down, down, into a deep dark tunnel.

'What do you want from me?' Sam whimpered.

This time, however, Tom Tiddler remained silent. Sam felt the pressure on his eyes disappear. The fingers were gone. Scarcely daring to look, Sam peeked through the crack in one eye. What he saw made no sense. He opened both eyes, and stared round him in horror. Everything had changed.

The outer edge of the clearing was now marked with a picket fence. Inside it was a circle of carefully tended garden beds. Where the dark brown earth had been – so totally devoid of life – now there were flowers and vegetables, fruit trees and bushes of sweet-smelling herbs.

Sam took a step backwards. The ground

wobbled. He looked down, and found he was standing on planks of wood which had been laid carefully on the ground in a ring – the grey ring, Sam remembered – to protect visitors' feet from the thick, squelchy mud underneath.

'Where am I?' Sam whispered, looking round. At the very centre of the garden – where the black inner circle had been – was a small, round, ramshackle hut. And in the doorway, stood Tom Tiddler.

'Something found and something lost,
You pay the price, you count the cost.
Something lost and something found –
You be in Tom Tiddler's Ground.'

Sam stared, open-mouthed. It wasn't the verse – Sam was getting used to the riddling, rhyming way the little man spoke. It was Tom Tiddler himself. He, too, had changed.

His legs were no longer twisted and the hump had disappeared. He was a young man – perhaps twenty or twenty-one – with bright blue eyes, curly black hair and a set of strong white teeth. Although short for a man, there was nothing at all disproportionate about his body. If it hadn't been for the beard, Tom Tiddler might have been a boy of eleven or twelve.

'But . . .' said Sam.

Tom Tiddler silenced him with a finger to the

lips. He nodded towards an apple tree and mimed a figure crouching down.

'You want me to hide?' said Sam.

Tom Tiddler nodded. Then he raised his hand. There was something else. He tapped his finger against his right eye, against his right ear, against his right temple. Sam understood. Look, listen, remember. I certainly will! he thought. I've *got* to know what's going on.

Scarcely two minutes had gone by when Sam heard the gate in the picket fence open. Taking care not to be seen, he peered round from behind the tree.

There was a young girl at the gate. Pale and thin, she couldn't have been more than ten. Her hair was fair, matted; her eyes, small and suspicious. Around her shoulders was a ragged red shawl which she clutched to herself with bony, bruised arms. Her face was dirty. Her feet were bare. She limped across the planks of wood.

Tom Tiddler walked towards her.

'Please, sir,' said the girl. 'You have to help me!'

Tom Tiddler motioned for her to explain and, as the girl started talking, he listened carefully to every word; now nodding in sympathy, now shaking his head in dismay. Sam, too, listened as the girl told her tale.

Her name was Agnes; Agnes Sharples. She was thirteen years of age, the eldest of seven children. Her father was dead, her mother an alcoholic. They lived together in one damp room, existing on whatever the five oldest children managed to steal. When they did well, the family ate. When they did badly, she – Agnes – was beaten.

'Sometimes so badly I can hardly walk,' she said, and lifted her tattered skirt to show the extent of the bruising.

Tom Tiddler raised his hand. She should stop now. Sam saw that there were tears in his eyes.

The girl did not stop, though. She could not. She, too, was crying. Big wet tears slid down her cheeks, streaking through the grime. 'There are *two* things a pickpocket needs,' she sobbed. 'Nimble fingers and fast legs.' She hobbled closer to Tom Tiddler. 'Fast legs,' she wailed. 'All I can do is beg. And who wants to give money to me?'

Again, Tom Tiddler raised his hand. Again, the girl ignored his pleas for her to be still. She sniffed, and wiped her nose with her shawl.

'Who will give money to a beaten girl? A beaten girl is a bad girl. And you do not reward badness!' She sniffed. 'And so,' she said, more quietly now, 'I must go home. Empty-handed.' She paused. 'And be beaten again.'

For a third time, Tom Tiddler raised his hand. This time the girl was quiet. He patted the air. She should wait. He turned, lifted the latch and went inside the hut.

When Sam saw Tom Tiddler disappearing *down* a ladder into a dug-out basement, he realized that the hut was far bigger on the inside than it appeared from the outside.

Sleeping underground must be warmer in winter, Sam guessed.

As Tom Tiddler's head reappeared, Sam ducked back down. He watched the little man approach the girl. There was something in his hand. For a moment Sam panicked. He remembered the knife in his nightmare. What was Tom Tiddler about to do now?

With a flourish, he opened his hand. Sam craned his neck to see what was there. It was OK. There, lying on a silk handkerchief in the palm of his little hand, was a small pile of coins.

'Thank you!' the girl whispered, as he slipped the money into her cupped hands. 'Thank you.'

'Some for now, to keep your mother
    sweet –
And more for later, till you find your
    feet.'

So saying, he reached into his pocket and pulled out a necklace: a diamond necklace that sparkled like fire in the midday sun.

'But I can't!' the girl gasped.

'Take it!' said Tom Tiddler. 'Turn it into money.'

Speechless, the girl clasped the necklace to her chest. Tears welled up in her eyes.

'I don't . . .' she sniffed. 'What should I say. No-one has ever been so . . . so kind . . .'

Tom Tiddler smiled warmly. He took her bony hands in his own, and squeezed them gently.

Use it well – and may your life be sweet as honey!'

The girl sniffed again and dried her eyes. Turning to go, she paused and looked back. 'I'll never *ever* forget you,' she said.

When Sam saw the girl leaving, he emerged from his hiding place. But Tom Tiddler turned, raised his hand and patted the air again. Sit down! Wait! There is more to come.

Sam crouched back down. And, as the sun passed slowly across the sky that afternoon, four more children arrived in turn. Thomas Willoughby, Edwin Marwood, Eliza Bates and Mildred Bingham. Each one called for Tom Tiddler. Each one told a tale more dreadful than the last. And each one was sent on his or her way with a handful of hope: loose change for today and jewels for a new tomorrow.

The shadows were lengthening when the last child arrived. His name was Jack Coleridge and, like the others, he too had heard the rumours going round of a hermit who lived in the centre of the forest. A hermit who was there for those children who had no-one else to turn to. At first he had dismissed the stories as silly wishful thinking. After all, why should anyone help him? A chimney sweep's boy. An urchin.

But when the blisters on his hands turned septic, and his knees had become so swollen he could no longer climb the chimneys – and his father had strapped him for his laziness – Jack decided to run away and see for himself.

As Tom Tiddler placed the riches in his hand, Jack looked up. Like the others, there were tears in his eyes. Like the others, he thanked Tom Tiddler and promised that he would never *ever* forget him.

Sam watched the boy leave. He wondered whether that was it; whether Tom Tiddler considered that he had seen enough. It was already beginning to get dark.

All at once, Tom Tiddler turned and glared at him. He was clearly furious.

'What?' said Sam.

'We'll always remember! We'll never forget!'

he said, his high-pitched voice bitter and mocking.

'The lies that such ingrates beget!' he
   shouted.
'We'll never forget! We'll always
   remember! –
Remember, remember, the fifth of
   November!'

All at once, the entire garden was plunged into darkness. It was as if someone had switched off the sun. Sam stepped forward, stumbled and tripped. Once again, he was falling.

Down, down, into the darkness.

CHAPTER TWENTY-ONE

When the falling sensation finally stopped, Sam opened his eyes. He had been praying that the strange garden, the ramshackle hut and Tom Tiddler himself would all have disappeared. The good news was that they had. The bad news was that so had everything else! No longer outside at all, Sam found himself lying on a settee in a completely unknown room.

Where am I? he wondered, looking around.

The room was warm, but not what you'd call cosy. The floorboards had been stripped and varnished, and there were wooden Venetian blinds at the window. One wall was a collage of framed sepia photographs; the others were bare. Even the smell was wrong. At home, there was a lingering smell of stewed tea and soap powder. Here, the air smelt of joss sticks and pine smoke.

He looked up through the large bay window. There was a holly tree, and beyond that, a wide expanse of green. 'St George's Park!' Sam exclaimed, jumping to his feet. 'This must be—'

'You're awake!' said a voice from behind him.

Sam spun round. 'Jordy!' he said.

'Are you all right?' said Jordy, as she hurried across the room. 'I just didn't know what to do. One minute you were standing there, and the next—'

Sam looked at Jordy. She was close to tears. He knew he must have given her quite a fright.

'I'm sorry, I—' he said.

'I couldn't tell whether you'd fainted or knocked your head . . .' she said tearfully.

'I'm all right now,' said Sam. Her tears were making him feel awkward. 'Don't cry.'

'You looked asleep,' she said, sobbing still louder. 'Just asleep. But I couldn't wake you. I waited for about an hour, but . . . you just wouldn't wake up!'

Sam leant forward and hugged her clumsily. 'I'm all right, now,' he said again.

'That's when I came to get Grandmother,' she sniffed, and pulled away. 'I was terrified you wouldn't be there when we got back . . .'

'But I was,' said Sam. Jordy nodded, and

94

swallowed. 'And if it wasn't for you,' he said. 'I'd still be there now.'

'If it hadn't been for me you wouldn't have been there in the first place!' said Jordy.

'Is that the invalid I can hear?' came a voice from the hall.

"S my grandmother,' Jordy said.

At that moment, a tall, red-haired woman wearing a baggy jumper and tight leggings strode into the room. 'Prudence,' she said, taking Sam's hand and shaking it vigorously. 'Prudence Carraway. But you can call me Pru.' She turned to Jordy. 'And I'd be grateful if you'd do the same,' she said. 'I've asked you often enough.'

'Grandmother doesn't like being called Grandmother,' said Jordy, grinning cheekily.

'It's the word, you see,' said Pru. 'Once people hear you're a grandmother, they assume you're old and grey,' she said. 'Which I am not!'

Sam nodded. She was right. Even though he knew that she was writing a book and lived in a house that looked like something out of a magazine, when Jordy had mentioned her 'grandmother', Sam had indeed imagined a little old lady with a cardigan, sensible shoes and a perm.

'Not that I've anything against grand-mothers,' Pru continued. 'I just hate being pigeonholed.'

Again, Sam knew what she meant. *He* hated

95

being lumped together with everyone else of his age. 'The youth of today!' *his* grandmother would complain, as if they were all one huge, monstrous yob.

'I've just made some camomile tea,' said Pru. 'Would you both like a cup?'

Sam looked at Jordy for help. He had no idea what camomile tea was. Jordy nodded. Sam looked back at Pru and said that, yes, he'd like some, too. And as Pru headed back to the kitchen, he and Jordy followed her.

'So,' said Pru, as she poured the tea into mugs, and stirred in some honey. 'You've made a full recovery. Have you any idea what happened to you in the woods?'

Sam shrugged. He was unsure how much he should say. Part of him wanted to tell her everything. After all, because of her research, Prudence Carraway probably knew more about Tom Tiddler than anyone else. He began to explain but, embarrassed by how weird it all sounded, Sam soon clammed up. He didn't want her to think he was crazy!

Pru's next question, however, was so direct that Sam had no choice but to answer. Yes, he *did* think there was a connection between Tom Tiddler and his nightmares!

The relief of admitting it to someone else was overwhelming. Sam found himself pouring his heart out. About the clearing that he had somehow 'known' was there; about the hideous dwarf and the bearded boy; about his trip back into the past – if that's what it had been. About everything!

'You don't think I'm mad, do you?' he said, when he was finished.

Prudence Carraway shook her red hair. 'No!' she said. 'I don't. Tell me that final rhyme again.'

Sam cleared his throat. ' "We'll always remember! We'll never forget! The lies that such ingrates beget." What are ingrates?' he said.

'People who are ungrateful,' said Pru.

'And beget?' said Jordy.

'To produce as an effect,' said Pru. 'To cause. This . . . this . . . I don't like the term "dwarf": it degrades people of diminished stature. This *vertically challenged* individual is clearly angry that none of the children kept their promise to remember him. Intriguing!' She turned back to Sam. 'And the last bit,' she said.

'We'll never forget! We'll always remember!' Sam recited. 'Remember, remember, the fifth of November!'

Pru nodded. 'Someone . . .' She paused. 'Or something – is trying to make contact with you,' she said. 'That much is clear. And using your nightmares to do it . . .'

'But Tom Tiddler *is* the nightmare,' Sam protested.

'I wonder?' said Pru thoughtfully. 'Perhaps it

97

was the nightmares you were already having which led him to you.'

'You're both talking as if Tom Tiddler's a real person,' said Jordy. 'It's only something from a game.'

'Jodie, I'm surprised at you!' said Pru. 'You know full well that *all* games have their origins in reality. The bogeymen in the variations of the *Tom Tiddler* games have always been derived from some famous – or infamous – character or other. It's just a matter of discovering who.'

'So you don't know anything about this Tom Tiddler,' said Sam disappointedly.

'I'm afraid not,' said Pru. 'But I'll tell you what,' she added, brightly, 'I soon shall!'

Sam smiled. Without knowing why, he had absolute confidence in Prudence Carraway. The next moment, however – as Pru looked up at the calendar – that confidence was cruelly shattered.

'The fifth of November!' Pru gasped. 'That's this coming Friday.' She looked at Sam. 'Let's just hope I can find out all I need in the local museum,' she said.

Yes, let's! thought Sam. The sooner he got some answers, the happier he would be.

CHAPTER TWENTY-TWO

It was half-past six when Sam finally got back home.

'Sam!' his mum exclaimed as he walked in the door. 'Are you all right, darling? Mrs Carraway phoned. Said you'd taken a bit of a tumble.' She squeezed his upper arm, his lower arm; she massaged his fingers. 'Nothing broken, at least,' she said, and placed her hand against his forehead.

Sam pulled away. 'I'm OK, Mum,' he said.

'But what happened?' she said.

'I was helping Jordy find her dog. In the woods, and—'

'And you climbed a tree. And you fell! How many times have I got to tell you?'

Sam nodded. If his mum wanted to think he'd fallen out of a tree, then that was fine by him.

'Oh, if anything should ever happen to you . . .' she said, and shuddered. 'Go up and have a nice warm bath.'

'But I—' Sam began.

'No arguments,' she said. 'You'll feel tons better.'

Five minutes later, Sam had to admit that it *did* feel good lying in the hot, soapy water. The whole experience in the woods had left him feeling dirty. As he wiped himself with the flannel and dunked his head underwater, it was like rinsing away the nightmare itself.

Sam's head was still under the water when he heard his dad slamming the front door shut. He was not happy! Sam surfaced and listened.

The problem was money. Again! What else? The bank had turned down his dad's application for a loan.

'Well, what did you expect?' his mum said. 'You can hardly use the house as security. We haven't paid the mortgage for six months and . . .' Sam sank back under the water. 'Blob blob blob blob blob!'

'Give me a break!' he muttered. With his ears submerged, Sam did not recognize his own voice. It was loud, deep – and oddly nasal. He began humming a nursery rhyme quietly to himself. Under the water, it sounded as though he was standing in an echoing cathedral.

Half a pound of tuppenny rice. Half a pound of treacle . . . The humming completely drowned out his parents' angry voices. *That's the way the money goes. POP!* Sam stuck his head out of the water. The shouting had stopped.

'. . . goes the weasel!' he said softly.

Cold and pruney, Sam finally got out of the bath an hour later. He grabbed a towel and rubbed himself down. Then, with his toothbrush in one hand, he began wiping the condensation off the mirror with the other. The next instant Sam froze in horror. The eyes staring back at him were not his eyes. The face in the mirror was not his face.

'Y . . . y . . . you,' he stammered, the blood pounding in his temples.

The toothless mouth grinned.

'Sometimes awake, sometimes asleep,
Into your life, Tom Tiddler will creep.'

'But why?' Sam shouted. 'What do you want?'

The creature did not reply. Then, as Sam stood there, transfixed, the face suddenly changed. In place of the hideous monster, was the bearded young man. His

101

mischievous blue eyes twinkled; the mouth broke into a smile – and was gone. The ugly creature, all hump and warts, had returned.

'What's going on?' Sam wailed.

Back and forth they went. Now the hideous dwarf. Now the bearded boy. Faster and faster, until the reflection in the mirror was a flickering blur.

Sam stepped back. 'Are you *both* Tom Tiddler? I don't understand,' he said, dizzily.

The flickering came to an abrupt halt. Sam found himself looking at the younger version. The mouth smiled.

> 'Sometimes asleep, sometimes awake,
> Until you have what you shall take.'

And with that, he vanished. Sam cupped his head in his hands; he rubbed his eyes with trembling fingers. The appearance of the two Tom Tiddlers had left him feeling frightened and alone. He needed to tell someone what he had seen.

If only I could talk to Mum and Dad, he thought. But Sam knew that was out of the question. They both had far too much on their plates already. Still, Pru had invited him for Sunday lunch the following day. Sam would just have to wait until then.

He sighed and looked up. His own face stared back at him from the mirror.

'You look awful!' said Sam to his reflection.

'I know,' he replied.

CHAPTER TWENTY-THREE

At ten o'clock the following morning, Sam was already on Jordy's doorstep, knocking lightly at the door. He knew it was early; far too early for lunch. But he couldn't wait a moment longer. Even though he hadn't had the nightmare again, the memory of the two faces had not gone away. Why had they both appeared? And what was it they wanted him to have? Sam *had* to talk to someone. And as soon as possible. He knocked again, more loudly.

Rapper started barking, and it soon became obvious that the dog was the only one awake in the house. Sam was unsure what to do. Even if his knock hadn't woken them, Rapper certainly would have by now. He was on the point of creeping away, when the door suddenly clicked open, and a bleary-eyed Prudence Carraway peered out.

'Hello!' she said. 'Here for breakfast too, are you?'

Sam felt his face turn red. 'I've had breakfast,' he said.

Pru laughed. 'Come in,' she said, wrapping her kimono tightly around her. 'I'm afraid we're not very early risers in this house.' She padded over to the foot of the stairs. 'Jodie,' she called. 'Jodie, it's Sam!'

There was silence.

'Jodie!' she called again.

'All right!' came the irritated reply.

Pru turned to Sam and smiled. 'Not at her best in the morning, our Jodie,' she said. 'She'll be better after a bowl of muesli. Why don't you wait in the sitting room? I'll go and chivy her along.'

'OK,' said Sam.

The sitting room was dark. Sam opened the blinds and sat down on the settee. On the coffee table in front of him was a personal stereo; beside it, an empty cassette box.

'*The Rhine Maidens*,' he read. 'Never heard of them.'

He slipped the headphones over his ears and pressed 'play'. Instantly, his head was filled with a cacophony of wailing women's voices against a background of violins and a drum machine. Sam winced. It was horrible. Truly horrible.

Surely Jordy can't like this stuff, he thought, and laughed to himself. And she thinks *I'm* weird!

Suddenly, Sam froze. *It* was happening again. The music had stopped, and instead, he heard a voice; a high-pitched, nasal voice. The voice of Tom Tiddler.

'The house for me is the house for you –
In the dusty attic, 'neath number two.
The house for you was the house for
me –
A treasure map that I want you to see.'

Message over, the music abruptly started up again. Staring into mid-air, Sam reached up slowly, pulled the headphones off and lay them in his lap. The drum machine continued to beat – tchii-tchii-tchii. In the kitchen, Rapper was howling.

Sam was still staring ahead five minutes later, when Jordy walked into the room. She took one look at Sam, and panicked.

'What is it?' she cried, rushing over and kneeling down beside him.

Sam looked at her, but said nothing.

'You look as though you've seen a ghost!' she said.

106

Sam shook his head miserably. 'Not "seen",' he said. 'Heard!'

Jordy looked down at the tape box. '*The Rhine Maidens*!' she said. 'I'm not surprised you look pale. They're awful! Pru loves them, of course. I make her listen to them on the Walkman.'

Sam smiled weakly. 'It wasn't the music,' he said. 'It was Tom Tiddler.'

Jordy nodded. 'Rapper knew again,' she said, quietly. 'It must be some kind of sixth sense . . . Did he say anything new?'

'Yes,' said Sam, and fell silent.

'Well?' said Jordy.

Sam breathed deeply. 'Something about a treasure map!' he said.

Jordy stared at him. 'A treasure map,' she said finally. 'You're not making this up, are you?'

'Making it up?' Sam shouted, and jumped to his feet. 'If that's what you think, I might as well go now.'

Jordy grabbed his arm. 'I'm sorry, Sam. I do believe you. Of course I do,' she said.

'Good!' said Sam angrily. ''Cos if you don't . . .' He swallowed. 'No-one else is going to.'

'I didn't mean it,' said Jordy. 'Honest. It's just that . . . well, I mean, a treasure map! It's so *boy*ish!'

'But that's the whole point,' said Sam. 'Tom Tiddler's just like a boy. Apart from the beard, he *is* a boy. Well, half the time, anyway,' he

107

added, and shuddered at the thought of the hideous hunchback.

'So, where is it, then?' said Jordy. 'This treasure map?'

Sam shook his head. 'I'm not sure. See what you make of it,' he said. He closed his eyes, and repeated Tom Tiddler's latest rhyme as best he could. 'I think that was it,' he said, looking up.

Jordy was staring at him in horror. *'The house for you was the house for me,'* she said. 'He must have lived at your address.'

'That's what I thought it meant,' said Sam flatly.

'But that's terrifying!' she said. 'You're being *haunted*! Shall I ask Pru if you can sleep over tonight?'

'No,' said Sam. 'I'll be all right. I don't know why, but . . . ever since I saw the younger Tom Tiddler . . . I mean, it still makes me jump when he appears . . .' He paused. 'Anyway, what if there *is* a treasure map there . . . ?'

'Well, you're braver than I am,' said Jordy.

''Course, I'll have to wait till Mum and Dad are out,' Sam continued. 'The loft's out of bounds.'

Jordy laughed. 'Or just more stupid!' she said.

CHAPTER TWENTY-FOUR

When Sam had discovered that Pru was a vegetarian, he'd groaned inwardly. He had been hoping that 'Sunday lunch' meant what it had used to mean in the Dillon household. Roast chicken, or pork, or beef and Yorkshire pudding. But no. It was more beans and lentils!

But as he took a bite of the Cashew Nut Bake, as Pru called it, a huge grin spread all over his face.

'It tastes so *meaty*!' he said.

Pru laughed. 'Haven't you eaten vegetarian food before?' she said.

'All the time!' Sam moaned. 'But it doesn't taste anything like this!' he added, realizing that he must have sounded a bit rude.

'I'll give you a copy of my recipe book,' she said. 'It's called *The Reluctant Vegetarian*.' She smiled. 'For people who don't want to eat meat, but can't do without the taste! Any more for any more?' she said.

'Please!' said Sam, eagerly holding his plate out.

'Pru-uu!' said Jordy.

'Ye-es?' said Pru.

'Oh, nothing,' said Jordy.

'It must have been something,' said Pru.

'It's just . . . Can I have an advance on my allowance?'

'Persuade me,' said Pru.

Jordy looked down, and began streaking the gravy with her fork. 'I just . . . need some.'

Pru lay her cutlery down on her plate, patted her lips with her napkin, and looked up.

'This wouldn't have anything to do with fireworks, would it?' she said. 'You know what I think about them.'

'Oh, go on, Pru,' said Jordy. 'It's only once a year.'

'Absolutely not,' said Pru. 'And you won't get round me by calling me by my proper name for once. I am not giving you money for you to go and burn it!'

'But—'

'Besides, I do not approve of celebrating the taking of a life. You know that.'

110

'Oh, Grandmother!' said Jordy angrily. 'It's a tradition.'

'So is the Solstice Dance, but where were you on Midsummer's Day?' said Pru.

'You mean I can't have my allowance just because I refused to prance around on a hill in the middle of the night with a load of old hippies?'

'An allowance is precisely that,' said Pru, standing up from the table. 'Money that *I* allow *you* to have.'

'It's *my* money!' Jordy shouted. 'Mum and Dad left it to me!'

Sam knew that if he had talked to his parents like that he'd now be halfway upstairs to his bedroom, and probably nursing a throbbing ear. But Pru did not react in the same way. The angrier she became, the more quietly she spoke.

'If you must waste money on sticks of gunpowder,' she said, 'then do what I had to do as a girl. Make a guy, go out, and earn it.'

'Fantastic,' said Jordy sarcastically. 'I'm sure they'd love to hear that you're sending me out begging now!'

Prudence Carraway stared at her granddaughter for a second. The pain in her eyes was unmistakable. Then she turned and left the room. Sam looked at Jordy. She was staring down at her plate defiantly. The next moment, she leapt up and rushed after her grandmother.

111

Sam heard the sound of sobbing apologies and *I-didn't-mean-its* coming from the kitchen. He hadn't liked to ask why Jordy was living with her grandmother. He knew she'd tell him in her own good time. Now he knew anyway.

Her parents were both dead.

CHAPTER TWENTY-FIVE

'Why didn't you tell me?' said Sam.

'I don't think about them that often,' said Jordy. 'And when I do, it's only the photographs I remember.'

Head down, Jordy was threading elastic through a length of old lace. She paused. Sam looked up from the hat that he was decorating with a feather and a band. He decided not to say anything. Finally, Jordy continued.

'I was almost two when it happened,' she said. 'A plane crash.' She paused again, and gathered the material to make a circular concertina shape. 'They'd gone to New York. For their wedding anniversary. They'd left me with Pru . . .'

She tied a knot in the ends of the elastic, and waved the finished article under Sam's nose.

'There!' she announced. 'One Jacobean ruff.'

Sam nodded. 'And you're still with her,' he said softly.

'Yes,' said Jordy. 'And I'm sorry we argued, Sam . . .'

'I'm used to it,' said Sam with a shrug.

Using two pairs of old tights (one for the legs and one for the head), a sweatshirt and waistcoat (for the body and arms) a velvet curtain (for the cloak), plus the lace ruff, an old pair of ankle boots and a wig of long black wool, Jordy supervised the construction of the best guy Sam had ever seen.

'It's brilliant,' he said.

'All we need is a mask, and presto! Mr Guy Fawkes himself,' said Jordy.

Even Pru was impressed, despite herself – although she did insist that the velvet curtain be removed *before* the guy made its way on to any bonfire.

'It's a pity it's raining,' said Pru. 'Otherwise you could go out now.'

Sam looked at his watch. 'I said I'd be back by five anyway,' he said. 'Tomorrow? After school?'

'If it's not still raining,' said Jordy.

'Even if it is,' said Sam. 'We leave it much longer, and there aren't going to be any fireworks left.'

'Yes,' said Pru, darkly. 'We've got a lot to do before the fifth of November.'

Sam arrived home half an hour later, soaked to the skin. As he turned the key in the lock and pushed the door open, he noticed something strange. The house was silent.

'Mum?' he called. His voice echoed round the half-decorated hallway. 'Dad?' Again, there was no answer. Both his parents were out.

Forgetting about his wet clothes, Sam raced upstairs. He pulled the aluminium step-ladder out from under his parents' bed and set it up under the loft-hatch. Then, with the torch in his mouth, he climbed the ladder, lifted the cover and pulled himself up into the roof space.

Balancing on the wooden joists, Sam shone the torch around the dark, triangular room. Shadows spun like giant bats. Sam trembled. There was something metallic about the air.

The torchlight came to rest on a pile of boxes in the centre of the room. Each was neatly labelled with a description of its contents. *Photo albums, 56-68, Photo albums, 90-93, Christmas Decorations, Sam's Toys, 0-5* – next to which was Sam's first bike. He rang the Mickey Mouse bell, and remembered how proud he'd been of it – how wonderful it had felt to ride without stabilizers for the first time.

Sam sighed and wondered whether the days

115

of new bikes were gone for ever. Then again, he thought, why was he in the loft? Answer: To find the treasure map. Of course, he was going to be able to buy a new bike – *and* a new car for his mum and dad!

'Where are you?' he muttered, as he stepped gingerly over the joists, shining the light into each and every crack and crevice. 'Where *are* you?' he said.

And then he saw it. Scratched into the bricks above both main beams was a Roman numeral – I and III. Sam shone the torch up the other end of the loft. II and IV. It must have been something the original builders had done. Taking care not to slip, Sam crossed the joists to the number two. And sure enough, at the point where the beam was sunk in the bricks, the same number had been scratched into the wood.

''Neath number two!' said Sam, crouching down to look under the beam.

He shone the light into the gap between brick and wood, and there – as clear as anything, when you knew where to look – was lodged a small, folded piece of yellowed paper. With a trembling hand, Sam slid his fingers as far into the crack as they would go, and began teasing the paper out with his nails.

'Got it!' he exclaimed.

The next moment, Sam's triumph turned to panic. Someone was in the house. He could hear them moving about downstairs. It was his mum and dad – back from wherever they'd been.

'Oh, no!' Sam muttered, as he hurried as fast as he could for the hatch. 'Oh, no! Oh, no!'

Being in the loft was a groundable offence, and Sam did not intend to be grounded! Not with Firework Night coming up. With arms shaking and heart pounding, he grabbed hold of the side of the hatch and began lowering himself down onto the ladder.

'I think it's upstairs,' he heard his dad saying.

OH, NO! thought Sam.

'Are you sure it's not in the shed?' his mum suggested.

Yes, yes, thought Sam, as he slotted the cover back into place as quietly as he could. Go and look in the shed.

But his dad was not convinced. 'I'm sure I saw it next to the cases,' he said, and Sam heard him crossing the hallway beneath him.

There wasn't time to replace the ladder – or even to collapse it – so Sam pushed it hurriedly into his bedroom and over to the shelves built into the alcove. He heard his dad pounding up the stairs. Sam climbed the ladder and began poking around on the top shelf. Outside, he heard an irritated 'blast!' The next moment, his dad's head appeared round the door.

'Sam, you haven't . . .' He stopped, and looked up. 'What *are* you doing?' he asked.

'I was . . . errm . . . I'm looking for my protractor,' said Sam. 'I need it for tomorrow.'

'Why should it be up there?' said his dad, not entirely convinced.

Sam shrugged. 'It isn't anywhere else,' he said.

'Hmmph. Well, mind you don't scratch the paintwork when you put the ladder back,' he said. 'And by the way, have you seen the torch?'

Feeling himself begin to blush, Sam turned away and continued his search for the non-existent protractor. 'No, sorry, Dad – I haven't,' he said. Having the ladder out was one thing. Having the ladder out *and* the torch in his pocket was another. His dad was bound to be suspicious!

'Perhaps it *is* in the shed,' he said, and left.

With his dad out of the way, Sam climbed down the ladder. He closed his door, and pulled the piece of paper from his back pocket. Then, having cleared a space, he placed it on his desk and began unfolding it, bit by bit. The paper was old, fragile, and Sam had to take great care to to tear it.

'Easy does it,' he whispered to himself.

As he came to the final crease, he saw that something had been written. The ink had faded, and the writing itself was difficult to read.

'The . . . Treasure Map of . . . Tom Tiddler,' said Sam.

He unfolded the two halves of paper, and smoothed his hand down the crease. As he did so, his heart sank. It wasn't a map at all. At least, not your usual type – although, as Sam discovered as he ran his fingers along the words – it *did* seem to be giving directions.

Start at Cut Purse Corner
Where two sovereigns greet the day.
One shall line your pocket,
The other point the way.

Follow, then, her finger,
Until the church you reach.
Look inside the graveyard
For the angel who did teach.

Examine with great caution,
Examine with great stealth.
For one wing leads to nothing,
The other leads to wealth.

Proceed in this direction,
For ten score yards and three.
Ignoring all obstruction
Until you find the tree.

Climb into its branches;
Heaven awaits you there.
A fork, that never graced a table,
Holds the costliest fare.

Sam groaned. Being able to read the words was one thing. Understanding them was another. He read through the verses again. It was no good. Sam hadn't a clue what the riddles meant.

CHAPTER TWENTY-SIX

When the final bell rang the following day, Sam and Jordy left school together. First stop was the newsagent's. There, they pooled their money and bought the best Guy Fawkes mask in the shop, and then headed back to Jordy's house.

With the mask in place, the guy was finally complete. It looked tremendous: lifelike and oddly menacing.

'What we need now,' said Sam. 'is an old pram or buggy – something to wheel it along in.'

Jordy grinned. 'I'd already thought of that,' she said. 'Come and see what I've got.'

Sam followed her out into the back garden. There, on the patio, was a doll's pushchair. 'I found it over the park last night,' she said, as she sat the guy into the seat. 'Or rather, Rapper did.'

'It's perfect,' said Sam, standing back to admire their handiwork. 'If this doesn't make us at least a tenner, I'll eat my hat.'

'What hat?' said Jordy.

'Well, my belt, then,' Sam laughed. 'Come on,' he said. 'I thought the High Street would be best. Outside the chemist's. Loads of people,' he added.

They walked back towards the centre of town. It was cold and windy, but at least it wasn't raining. As they passed the statue, Jordy turned to Sam.

'Did you manage to get up into your loft?' she said.

Sam slipped his hand into his back pocket. 'Here,' he said, handing her the copy of the verse he'd made. 'Though I don't think it'll mean much to you.'

Jordy read it through. And then again. She looked up. 'You're right,' she said. 'As we don't know where Cut Purse Corner is, it's impossible to know where to start. Why couldn't he have drawn a proper map?'

'And spoil all the fun?' Sam sighed.

'I'm sure Pru will find something out at the museum,' said Jordy. 'She's very thorough.'

Sam nodded glumly. If he was ever going to

buy that new bike – not to mention the car! – he
could only hope that Jordy was right.

There *were* a lot of people on the High Street.
Unfortunately, most of them passed by the two
children and their guy without even seeing them
– and the few who *did* notice kept their hands in
their pockets.

'Penny for the guy!' they shouted. 'Penny for
the guy.'

Half an hour later, and that was all they had
to show for their trouble. One penny! An old lady
had seen the guy, smiled, stopped, opened her
purse and pulled out the coin.

'There!' she beamed. 'And have a lovely
Firework Night.'

As she had disappeared back into the crowd,
Jordy and Sam had looked at each other and
burst out laughing.

'How were you thinking of eating that belt?'
said Jordy. 'Boiled, grilled or fried?'

'And how are we going to split the takings?'
said Sam.

'With a hacksaw!' said Jordy.

Sam shrugged. It was all very well laughing.
'What do you say we give up?' he said.

Jordy looked at her watch. 'Let's wait a few
more minutes,' she said. 'The offices empty out
at five o'clock.'

'OK,' said Sam. 'But it's Monday, remember.

No-one likes Mondays. That's why everyone's being so mean—'

'Sam!' Jordy interrupted excitedly.

'What is it?' said Sam.

'Look!'

Sam followed the line of her pointing finger. 'What?' he said.

'The statue,' said Jordy. 'It's Queen Victoria, isn't it?'

Sam looked at the figure at the middle of the roundabout. 'I think so,' he said. 'Why?'

'Where's that poem?' she said. 'Tom Tiddler's verse.'

Sam looked through his pockets. It wasn't there. '*You've* got it!' he said.

'Oh, yes,' said Jordy. She pulled it out of her jacket pocket and began reading. ' " Start at Cut Purse Corner where two *sovereigns* greet the day",' she said. 'Sovereign – queen. Geddit? "One shall line your pocket. The other *point the way*." See?'

Sam looked at the statue. Even though he passed it every day, he had never really noticed it before. On one hand, she was carrying an orb. In the other, she was holding up a sceptre. It was pointing down the High Street.

' "Follow, then, the finger,"' Jordy went on excitedly. 'To the church,' she said. 'The next clue must be in St Benedict's. An angel,' she said. 'It's probably some kind of gravestone.'

124

Sam grinned. 'What are we waiting for?'

Just then, a church bell chimed. At the same time, the door next to the chemist burst open and a stream of people began filing out on to the pavements from the first floor offices.

'Penny for the guy!' Sam shouted. Jordy joined in. 'Penny for the guy! Penny for the guy!'

It was hopeless. No-one gave them a second glance, let alone any money.

'What we need,' said Jordy, 'is a gimmick! Something to get them to look at us.'

Sam shook his head. 'We need *some* kind of help,' he said. 'Before they all go. I wish—'

All at once, they both heard a voice.

'Remember, remember the fifth of November!' it said.

They looked round.

'Who said that?' said Jordy.

The voice rang out again. 'Remember, remember the fifth of November!'

'It's the guy!' Sam gasped.

Jordy looked at him. 'The guy?' she said. 'But—'

'Remember, remember . . .' came the voice for a third time.

Sam and Jordy stared at the guy. There was no doubt. The words were coming from behind the mask. What was more, it was a voice Sam knew only too well.

'It's Tom Tiddler!' he whispered.

'. . . the fifth of November!' it cried still louder. 'But how?' said Jordy. 'And why can *I* hear it?'

Sam shrugged. 'I don't know,' he said. 'But you're not the only one.'

As the guy continued to shout its reminder to all and sundry passing by, the people began to stop. They turned, looked down at the ornate talking guy and smiled. A young woman with a yellow mac put her hand in her pocket and dropped a coin in Sam's waiting hat. He glanced in.

'It's a pound!' he whispered excitedly.

From that moment on, there was no stopping them. One by one, as the men and women filed past, they all dipped their hands in their pockets. The air was filled with the sound of coins chinking into the hat.

'Remember, remember the fifth of November!' the guy continued, over and over.

Sam stared with a mixture of joy and fear. He said they'd needed some help, but did that help have to come from Tom Tiddler? What was he playing at? What was he after?

As the hat became almost embarrassingly full, Sam noticed something else. In the electrical appliance shop opposite, the display of televisions had gone wild. The pictures had all disappeared behind a blizzard of snowy interference, and were now flashing and sparking ominously.

'It's doing it again,' said Sam. 'It happens whenever Tom Tiddler makes an appearance. The nightmares. In the mirror . . .' He crouched down next to the pushchair and whispered to the guy. 'It's all right now, thanks. We've got enough.'

But the guy would not stop. 'Remember, remember the fifth of November!' it screeched.

Jordy pointed to the traffic lights. They were flashing on and off. Now green. Now red. Now green again. Suddenly, the air was filled with the sound of screaming metal as a lorry collided with a bus. Sam turned to the guy.

'Tom Tiddler,' he shouted. 'Be quiet!'

Instantly, the voice fell silent. The next moment the sound of a wailing siren filled the air, as a police car – with blue light flashing – arrived on the scene and skidded to a halt just in front of them.

'Come on,' said Sam, stuffing the hatful of money into his backpack. 'Let's get out of here!'

And with that, they were gone; desperate to put as much distance as possible between them and the chaos Tom Tiddler had caused. Over the road they raced, down a side street and out on to Duke's Lane. It was only when he saw the church up ahead that Sam finally stopped.

'St Benedict's,' he said. 'The church in the riddle. Do you want to check the graveyard now?'

Jordy shook her head. 'It's too dark,' she said. 'Let's meet back here, tomorrow.'

'Before school,' said Sam.

Jordy nodded. 'Eight o'clock,' she said.

It was cold and crisp the following morning. Sam and his mum had never got round to returning to the charity shop and, for the first time that year, he almost felt tempted to put on the anorak – but only almost! With gloves on his hands and a scarf wrapped round his neck and mouth, Sam still shivered as he made his way along the slippery pavement.

As he approached the church, the bells began to chime – six . . . seven . . . eight times.

On the dot, thought Sam, as he went in through the gate. He looked around. 'Unlike some!' he muttered – and immediately saw that he was wrong.

Jordy *was* there. Leaning forward, she was reading one of the gravestones. Sam ducked down and tiptoed down the path, and up behind her.

'Boo!' he said.

Jordy leapt round. Her face was white. Seeing Sam, standing there, her fear instantly turned to anger. 'You idiot!' she shouted. 'Never frighten me like that again. Never!'

Sam immediately felt guilty. 'I . . . I'm sorry,' he said. 'I . . .' Tears were welling up in Jordy's

128

eyes. She was trembling. 'I didn't think—' he said.

'That's just it,' Jordy interrupted. 'You didn't think!' Her whole body shuddered. She hugged her jacket tightly around her. 'I hate graveyards,' she said quietly.

Sam looked away. What was it Jordy had said earlier? That he was 'thoughtful'? That he was 'sensitive'? Given what he had learnt about Jordy's parents, he could hardly have been less sensitive.

'I'm sorry,' he said again. They were the only words he could think of. Suddenly Sam saw the face of Tom Tiddler – the young Tom Tiddler – floating in front of him. Just for a second. But even in so short a time, Sam couldn't help but notice the sadness in his eyes. He swallowed. 'Very sorry,' he said.

Jordy nodded. 'Come on, then,' she said. 'We've got half an hour to find the right gravestone. Oh, and before I forget,' she added, sounding more like her old self again, 'Pru wondered whether you'd like to come to tea,' she said. 'I think she's got something to show you.'

'She found something!' said Sam. 'What?'

Jordy shrugged. 'She wouldn't tell me. But she had her serious face on!'

By the time the church bell tolled the half hour, it was clear that their search had been in vain. They had looked at each and every grave-stone. Not one answered the description.

'Back to the drawing board,' Sam groaned.

Jordy looked at him. She could see the disappointment on his face.

'We've gone wrong somewhere,' she said. 'But I'm sure we're on the right track – and we've still got three more days to go.'

Sam's spine tingled with icy anticipation. Three more days until *what*, though? he thought miserably.

130

CHAPTER TWENTY-SEVEN

'I still can't believe we made so much money yesterday,' Jordy said, as she and Sam walked back to her house after school. 'How much was it again?'

'Fifty-eight pounds and fifty-one pence,' said Sam.

'Incredible!' she said. 'I'll tell you what, though. You must not – repeat, *not* tell Pru how much we made.'

Sam nodded. 'We can't spend it all on fireworks.' He paused. 'I thought I'd put some towards a new jacket,' he said, and immediately wished he hadn't.

Jordy stared at him. 'I thought you thought you looked cool without a jacket,' she said slowly.

'Oh, I'm cool all right,' said Sam. 'Freezing, in fact.'

He'd been trying to make her laugh, but Jordy simply continued to stare.

'You have all of it,' she said at last.

'No!' shouted Sam angrily, and his scalp felt all hot and prickly. 'We get half each,' he said.

'But—'

'Fifty-fifty. Like we agreed,' he said.

They walked on in silence. Pru saw them walking past the window and went to the door.

'Hey,' she said. 'You both look as if you've found a penny and lost a pound.'

Sam snorted.

'It's nothing,' said Jordy. 'We've got a French test tomorrow,' she added.

'Ah, *la langue française* . . .' said Pru, and waltzed back into the house reciting something utterly incomprehensible.

Sam glanced round at Jordy, who raised her eyes to the ceiling, which made Sam snigger – a noise he managed to transform into a sudden coughing fit. Pru looked round.

'You could do with a spoonful of drosera,' she said.

'Drosera?' said Sam.

'A homeopathic remedy for coughs,' she explained. 'Absolutely wonderful! It comes from a plant – *drosera rotundifolia* – a type of sundew,' she said.

132

'Really?' said Sam, trying to sound interested. It was Jordy's turn to stifle a laugh.

'A beautiful plant,' Pru continued. 'The flowers are ordinary enough, of course. But the leaves! They're small and fleshy, round and red, and covered with long sticky hairs which curve inwards. Can you guess why?'

Sam shook his head.

'To catch flies,' said Pru. 'They're carnivores. Unlike me!' she added. 'Now, who's for supper? How's that appetite of yours, Sam?'

He grinned. 'I could eat a horse,' he said.

'Not here, you can't,' said Pru. 'I've made a cheese and asparagus quiche. It should be about ready by now.'

Once again, Sam was amazed by how tasty the meatless meal was.

'Delicious,' he mumbled. 'I wish you could come and cook at our house.'

Pru laughed. 'It's in the cookery book,' she said. 'I really must dig you out a copy. Anyway, if it's all right with you two, I'd like to go and finish off some work.'

Sam looked up. 'Jordy said you'd found out a little about Tom Tiddler,' he said.

'One or two things,' said Pru. 'I now know where he lived, and when. His real name was Thomas Merson – the "tiddler" bit must have come about because he was short.'

'And what did he do?' asked Jordy.

'Not sure yet,' said Pru. 'I photocopied some newspaper articles I found this afternoon. They're what I want to look at now . . . And I've laid out some bits and bobs in the front room,' she said. 'Have a look at them when you've finished eating.' And with that, she disappeared up to her study.

The moment they heard her door clicking shut, Jordy and Sam abandoned their meal and made for the sitting room. There on the coffee table was a pile of papers.

'Born 17 April 1870,' said Sam, as he read through the first of Pru's many pages of notes. 'Died 5 November 1892.'

'Listen to this,' said Jordy. 'It's from *The Times*. "17 April, 1883. Thomas Merson, of King Street, Banworth, has been found guilty of eight charges of theft and given an eight-year prison sentence. Merson, 13, was caught red-handed in the act of pickpocketing outside the Stagecoach Inn, in the centre of town. The area is so notorious for its crime rate that it is known locally as *Cut Purse Corner*" . . .'

Jordy looked up. 'The Stagecoach is that pub on the corner,' she said.

'I know,' said Sam. 'Next to the chemist's . . .'

'Just where we set up the guy,' said Jordy quietly.

Sam nodded. 'What else does it say?' he asked.

'It says . . .' said Jordy, finding her place. 'Here

134

we are. "It was revealed that the boy had been forced into a life of crime by his father, Josiah Merson, almost as soon as he could walk. In sentencing, Judge Watts made mention of the severity of the punishment. By forcing Merson to spend the rest of his childhood in prison, he was not only considering the victims of his crimes, but also the boy himself. 'He should grow to maturity free from the corrupting influence of his wicked father.'" Blimey!' said Jordy.

'Eight years for pickpocketing!' said Sam. He was beginning to feel nervous. The ghost or spirit – or whatever it was that had been contacting him – must have a pretty big chip on his shoulder. What if he's using *me* to get his own back? Sam wondered, and trembled at the thought. 'I wonder what *did* happen on November the fifth,' he said nervously.

'I don't know,' said Jordy quietly. 'But something tells me it wasn't nice!'

Sam walked to the other end of the room. He needed to clear his head. He pushed the window open and breathed in the cold night air.

'I'll be all right,' he told himself. He took another deep breath. 'Everything's going to be fine.'

'Hey! Sam,' called Jordy. 'Come and have a look at this.'

Sam returned to the table, where Jordy had spread out a large photocopy. Entitled *The*

Changing Face of Banworth, it was taken from a guide book of the town. There were two maps; one from 1880 and one from a hundred years later. It was interesting to see how big the town had grown; how the forest had shrunk – but Sam did not know why either should have excited Jordy quite so much.

'Not the maps,' she said, and pointed to a photograph of the statue of Queen Victoria on the opposite side. 'Notice anything?' she said.

Sam looked. It had been taken in 1936. In black and white. There were very few cars around . . . Sam shook his head.

'Look at the statue,' said Jordy, barely able to contain herself.

'Yes,' said Sam, looking. 'What about it?'

'Oh, for heaven's sake,' said Jordy, grabbing the paper back. 'Look,' she said. 'You see where the sceptre's pointing. Now look behind, on the right. What's that?'

'The Stagecoach,' said Sam. Suddenly, the penny dropped. 'She's pointing in a different direction!'

'Precisely!' said Jordy.

'But why?'

Jordy pointed to the text underneath. 'It says here,' she said, 'that when it was first erected, the town elders decided to have the queen pointing towards the north – the centre of indus-trial wealth. But,' she continued, ' "the statue was damaged during the second world war. When it was repaired, the then mayor had it turned so that she would be pointing, instead, to the centre of government." Typical!' she added.

'So St Benedict's wasn't the right church,' said Sam. 'It was . . .' He looked over at the map. 'St Luke's.'

Jordy grinned. 'Treasure, here we come!' she said.

At that moment, Pru burst into the room. Her face was white.

'What's the matter?' Jordy asked.

Tight-lipped, Pru shook her head. 'I don't like it,' she said. 'I don't like it at all.' She turned to Sam. 'I can't force you of course but, for your own safety, I don't think you should have anything further to do with this Tom Tiddler character.'

'But, but . . . I can't,' said Sam.

'Sam,' said Pru. 'I'm concerned. I think he might mean you harm.'

'Harm?' said Sam, trying to ignore the shivers shooting up and down his spine. 'Then why did he help us get all that money?'

Sam winced. It was the old problem. Foot and mouth disease. Every time he opened his mouth, he put his foot in it.

'What money?' Pru demanded.

'Oh, we did quite well with the penny-for-the-guy,' said Jordy lightly. She laughed. 'Sam's got

137

this crazy idea that Tom Tiddler had something to do with it.'

Pru looked horrified. 'He gave you money,' she gasped. 'But that's how it all starts!'

'How *what* starts?' Sam shouted.

Pru breathed in, and fixed Sam with her deep brown eyes. 'I don't want to . . . I *can't* tell you. For your own good. But I believe you have been drawn into something extremely dangerous. Please, please, from now on, try not to have anything to do with him – at least until I find out a little bit more.'

'But how?' said Sam. 'It's all on his terms.'

'Well, if he appears, just turn away,' said Pru. 'If he speaks, don't listen.' She shrugged. 'I don't know what else to suggest. All I know is this. If half of what I have read is true, then Thomas "Tiddler" Merson was a monster.'

Sam stared after Pru as she turned and left the room. He thought of the carnivorous plants she had described earlier. Suddenly, Sam knew exactly how the flies must feel when they found themselves stuck in the middle of something they couldn't escape. He turned to Jordy.

'Now what?' he said.

Before Jordy had a chance to answer, there was a hissing noise from the corner of the room. The two children spun round and stared at the television which had mysteriously switched itself on. Jordy grabbed Sam's arm.

'What's going on?' she said.

'I don't know,' Sam replied. 'But I'm glad you can see it too.'

Slowly, the snowy screen cleared, and Jordy and Sam found themselves staring at a short, bearded young man standing in the middle of a garden.

'Is that him?' said Jordy.

'The young one. Yes,' Sam nodded.

'He looks so sad,' said Jordy.

Sam nodded again. 'But perhaps Pru's right,' he said, and turned away.

As he did so, Tom Tiddler began to speak. Sam put his hands to his ears and began to hum. But it was no good. The voice filled his head: it would not be ignored.

> 'So many lies, so much deceit,
> The crimes that they lay at Tom
>   Tiddler's feet.
> So much deceit, so many lies.
> But the truth can never hurt the wise.'

Then the screen went dead.

Sam looked at Jordy. Jordy looked back at him.

'Well?' said Sam.' Do we trust him or not?'

Jordy shrugged. 'I don't think we've got much choice in the matter, either way,' she said. 'He's obviously not going to leave you alone.'

'*You* saw him, too,' Sam reminded her quietly. 'Whatever it is that Tom Tiddler wants, it involves both of us now.'

CHAPTER TWENTY-EIGHT

The following lunch-time, Jordy and Sam sat next to each other in the dining hall. They were trying to decide what they should do next. As usual, it was proving difficult to talk.

'You two getting married, or what?' Craig Martin demanded from the other side of the table.

Sniggers filled the air.

'Yeah,' added Billy. 'When's the big day?'

'Show us your ring!' taunted Niall.

'Ignore them,' Jordy said to Sam.

But Sam could not ignore them. There was enough going on without having to put up with Craig Martin and his two trained monkeys. He'd had enough!

Jumping up from his seat, Sam launched himself across the table, grabbed at Craig's jacket and pulled him to the floor. Then he hit him. Twice. Once to the chest. Once to the face. Fighting was easy, he thought.

The next instant, Craig pushed him hard in the jaw with the heel of his hand, and Sam found himself pinned down beneath the bigger boy. He wriggled. He struggled. Suddenly, his right leg was free, and he brought his knee up sharply. It thumped into Craig's stomach, winding him and sending him sprawling back over the floor. Sam jumped to his feet, and squared up.

'Come on, then,' he hissed through clenched teeth. 'Get up!'

Craig Martin, however, had had enough. He sat there on the floor, and rubbed his stomach tenderly. Someone at the back of the hall cheered. Within seconds, the entire dining hall was echoing with the whoops and cries of a hundred and eighty boys and girls who had just seen Banworth Junior's biggest bully finally getting a taste of his own medicine.

If *they* were happy about the fight, then Mr Barnes the headmaster was certainly not. When it had first begun, one of the dinner ladies had run along to his office. Now, he was standing in the doorway of the hall.

'BE SILENT!' he roared. 'Dillon! Martin! I want you both outside my office. Now!'

Sam winced. Mr Barnes was notorious for writing letters to parents about the behaviour of their sons and daughters. If he decided to write to *his* parents, it would probably arrive on the Friday morning. November the fifth; Firework Night!

Just my luck, Sam thought miserably.

Sam finally emerged from school at four o'clock. Jordy was waiting for him at the gates.

'Well?' she said. 'How did it go?'

Sam rubbed his bottom and winced theatrically. 'Six of the best,' he said.

'Seriously,' said Jordy.

Sam smiled. 'He was really nice. I told him everything that had happened . . . He said that what I'd done was wrong, but . . . what was it? "I cannot condone your actions, Samuel, understandable though they may have been".'

Jordy grinned. 'You've been let off!'

'Looks like it,' said Sam.

They walked on.

'He knew all about the chocolate business as well,' said Sam. 'He asked whether Craig had ever stolen any from me.'

'What did you say?' asked Jordy.

'I said "yeah, once or twice",' said Sam. He stopped and looked at Jordy. 'What else was I supposed to say?'

Jordy turned. 'You did right,' she said firmly.

143

'If Craig's in trouble, it's got nothing to do with the fight. Old Barnesy's obviously been watching him for some time.'

Sam nodded. 'That's what I thought,' he said.

'Anyway,' she said. 'We've got far more to worry about than Craig Martin.' She nodded towards the statue of Queen Victoria. 'Do we try St Luke's or not?'

Sam looked down at his feet. 'But . . .' he said.

'Pru need never know,' said Jordy. 'As long as you manage to keep quiet this time,' she added.

Sam remained silent.

'Look,' said Jordy. 'Nothing's going to happen. It's the day after tomorrow we've got to worry about. The fifth of November. Remember, remember?' she added, and grinned.

Sam smiled.

'And anyway,' Jordy continued. 'You heard what Tom Tiddler said. "The truth can never hurt the wise."'

Yes, thought Sam. But what if going to the church was *not* a wise thing to do? What if it turned out to be the most stupid thing he had ever done in his life?

'Come on,' said Jordy. 'Are you a man or a mouse?'

Sam looked up. 'Eeek eeek!' he squeaked, and grinned.

'OK,' he said. 'I will come and have a look. But the first sign of trouble, and we're out of there.

Agreed?'

'Agreed,' said Jordy.

As they went through the lych gate at the front of the church, both children fell silent. St Luke's was older than St Benedict's by several centuries, and much smaller. In contrast, its graveyard was more than twice the size.

Without speaking, the pair of them left the path, climbed the grassy bank and looked around them at the multitude of headstones – some of them recent, some dating back to the seventeenth century.

'You look at this end,' said Jordy. 'I'll start on the other side of the church, and we'll meet in the middle.'

Sam shook his head. 'There's no need,' he said. 'Look.'

As Jordy turned, she saw at once what Sam had noticed. Over by the far wall, one particular monument stood out from all the rest. Three times as high as the other gravestones, it consisted of a square plinth, tapering at the top, upon which stood a tall marble angel. In its left hand was an opened book, glinting orange in the light from the street lamp.

' "The angel who did teach",' said Jordy.

'Let's go and see,' said Sam.

A moment later, they were standing in front

145

of the monument. The inscription on the plinth confirmed that they had indeed found what they were looking for.

You taught us with generosity!
You awakened our curiosity!

Sam didn't know whether to be happy or sad. Half of him had been hoping they would draw a blank in the churchyard. Now, instead, they had solved the next part of Tom Tiddler's message. It meant making another decision.

Should they go on? Or should they quit while they still could?

CHAPTER TWENTY-NINE

In the end, of course, they had no choice. What had been started could not be stopped. Something more powerful than either Sam or Jordy was leading them, guiding them; steering them both towards a conclusion neither of them could have imagined in their wildest dreams – or their worst nightmares.

One by one, the clues fell into place. One wing pointed back to the east wall of the church, where a circular stained-glass window was framed in a giant stone *nothing*. The other pointed out of the churchyard, over the road, and into the woods beyond.

Sam and Jordy stood by the stile and peered into the trees. 'That's where the "wealth" must be,' said Sam. 'Down there somewhere.'

Jordy nodded. ' "Ten score yards and three", to be precise,' she said. 'About two hundred metres.'

'Hardly any distance at all,' said Sam.

'We could be there and back in a couple of minutes,' said Jordy.

Neither of them moved.

'So what are we waiting for?' said Jordy.

Sam shrugged. 'Nothing,' he said. 'It's just . . .'

'What?' said Jordy.

'I don't like that "heaven awaits you there" bit,' he said.

Jordy continued to stare into the woods. 'I thought that made it sound as if we were going to find something really good. You know, something we always wanted . . .'

Sam nodded. 'Could be,' he said. He paused. 'It could also be like, well . . .' he swallowed. 'Being dead.'

'So, do you think we should come back tomorrow?' said Jordy. 'When it's lighter?'

'Dark. Light. I don't think it makes much difference,' said Sam.

'Then, we may as well look now,' said Jordy logically.

Without saying a word, Sam climbed over the stile. He knew that, having come so far, there was no way that he was going to abandon the search. He *could* not. And since that was the case, then Jordy was right. It might as well be sooner than later.

'Soon be there,' he said, as they continued along the narrow, overgrown track. 'Are you still counting?'

'A hundred and eight. Yes. A hundred and nine,' she replied, and returned to counting the metres in her head.

Although night had by now fallen, and the trees were dense, enough moonlight was filtering through the branches for the children to walk without stumbling. Silver shadows sliced through the darkness. An owl hooted. Something scurried through the undergrowth. Jordy gasped. She seized Sam's arm and gripped it tightly.

'A hundred and seventy-six,' she said bravely. 'A hundred and seventy-seven. A hundred and seventy-eight.'

With every step, Sam felt his heart beating a little more quickly. He knew he was doing something wrong. If the loft was out of bounds, then the woods at night were an absolutely forbidden no-go area. If his mum and dad *ever* found out . . .

'A hundred and ninety-nine. Two hundred,' said Jordy. She stopped. Sam stopped beside her.

'I think my steps must have been a bit short,' said Jordy.

Sam nodded. 'There's a big tree up ahead,' he said, squinting into the darkness.

They walked on a little farther.

'Yes, look,' said Sam. 'This must be it. The path divides.' He looked up into the branches of the massive oak tree, and the words of Tom Tiddler's verse echoed round his head. 'Climb into its branches. Heaven awaits you there.' But what did it mean? 'Come on,' he said at last. 'Give me a leg up to that first branch. It should be easy after that.'

'You're *sure* you want to?' said Jordy.

Sam laughed. 'I wish you'd said that when we were back at the road,' he said.

'You *are* having second thoughts,' said Jordy.

'Second?' said Sam. 'I'm already up to *forty* second thoughts! Let's get it over with,' he said. 'Now we're here.'

Jordy bent down, and laced her fingers together. Sam lifted his foot. It hovered above Jordy's hands.

'Come on,' she said impatiently. 'Or do you want *me* to climb the tree?'

'No,' said Sam. 'I will.'

As Sam pushed down on the cupped hands, Jordy straightened up. Sam felt himself being propelled into the air. He reached up with his arms, hugged the huge branch above his head and heaved himself round onto it.

'Can you see anything?' Jordy called up.

150

'Not yet,' said Sam. 'I'll go a bit higher.'

From that first branch, the tree proved easy to climb. Footholds and handholds were all perfectly placed, and Sam soon found himself way up above the ground.

'Anything yet?' Jordy called again.

Sam shook his head, but said nothing. Confrontations with ghouls and fights with bullies were one thing; his fear of heights was another. Thankfully, in the dark, it was difficult to see just how high up he was.

Some ten metres above the ground, the main trunk divided. Sam, who was climbing up the outside branches at that point, noticed nothing at first. It was only when he put his foot into the fork in the tree, that he found himself standing on something *not* made of wood. 'Of course,' he whispered to himself. ' "A fork, that never graced a table." It's the fork of the tree.'

He looked down, but his own shadow plunged whatever it was into darkness. Easing himself round, Sam looked more closely. The corners of something metal glinted in the moonlight.

'I've found something!' he yelled.

'What?' came Jordy's voice from a long, long way below him.

'A box!' he shouted down. 'A strongbox!'

Sam tried to lift the lid, but the box was locked – and far too solid to be forced. There was a little oval of metal fixed to the front above

151

the keyhole by a screw. Sam pushed it to one side and fingered round the hole.

'It's locked!' he shouted. 'And there's no key.'

'Can you carry it down?' Jordy called back.

Sam braced his back against the bark, and tugged at the box. It didn't move. Closer inspection revealed that it *couldn't* move. Since it had been placed in the fork of the tree all those years ago, the bark and branches had both grown. Unable to dislodge the heavy rectangular object, they had grown around it, like the seaweed whose roots wrap themselves around rocks and stones. As time had passed, the tree had all but swallowed the box up. Whatever the 'costliest fare' inside was, it would have to wait. Disappointed, Sam climbed back down the tree.

'It's hopeless,' he said, as he landed with a thud next to Jordy. 'It'd take a chain-saw to break it free.'

'And you can't break it open?'

'Impossible,' said Sam.

'Well, how *are* we going to find out what's in it?' said Jordy, irritably.

'There's only one way,' said Sam. 'We'll have to find the key.'

Jordy groaned. 'And I bet I know who's got that,' she said.

They looked at one another. 'Tom Tiddler!'

CHAPTER THIRTY

'You know what we've forgotten,' said Sam the following day as, once again, they walked back to Jordy's house.

'What's that?' asked Jordy.

'Fireworks,' said Sam. 'All that money, and we haven't bought any fireworks yet.'

'If the expression on Pru's face was anything to go by, I think we're going to have fireworks enough, without buying any,' she said.

'Worried, is she?' said Sam.

'I've never seen her so worried,' said Jordy. 'God knows what she's discovered.'

'And she's definitely going to show us?' said Sam.

Jordy nodded. 'Like I said, she's had a change

of heart. I told her about Tom Tiddler appearing on the television,' she explained. 'And I think she now understands that we can't simply "turn away" and "not listen". So, she's decided to show us everything. "Forewarned is forearmed" as she put it.'

Sam looked at Jordy glumly. 'I hope she's not blaming me for getting you into all this.'

'I doubt it,' she said. 'Pru never blames *anyone* for *anything*. An armed robber? – his parents deprived him of cuddles! A mass murderer? – being smacked brutalized him!'

Sam laughed.

'She thinks Genghis Khan must have had a traumatic birth experience!' said Jordy.

By the time they reached the green door, the pair of them were aching with all the laughing. But as Jordy went to put the key in the lock, she turned and put her finger to her lips. 'Sssh!' she went. 'I don't want Pru to think we're not taking this seriously.'

'Is that you?' came Pru's voice, as Jordy turned the key and pushed the door open.

'Ye-es,' Jordy replied.

'I'm in my study,' Pru called. 'Come on up.'

Jordy looked at Sam and raised her eyebrows. 'We are honoured!' she said.

With Jordy in front, the two children went upstairs. Jordy knocked lightly on Pru's study door. It immediately flew open. 'There you are!' said Pru breathlessly. 'Come in.'

Sam found himself standing in a small room with a sloping ceiling. Most of the space was taken up with a huge desk. On it was a computer, keyboard and printer; a split level in-out tray, and a brass lamp, as well as numerous photocopies of documents, photographs, certificates and newspaper cuttings. It was one of these that Pru picked up. She looked around.

'Do sit down,' she said, taking the only chair in the room.

Jordy and Sam sat on the carpet, their backs leaning up against a couple of filing cabinets. They looked up expectantly. Pru stared back, first at Jordy, then at Sam.

'So,' she said. 'It's impossible to shut this . . . this apparition out, is it?'

'Completely,' said Sam. 'I tried, but—'

Pru raised her hand. 'Something else,' she said. 'Is there anything . . . peculiar about the way he speaks?'

'It's sort of nasal,' said Sam. 'And high-pitched . . .'

'Anything else? The words he uses, perhaps.'

Sam shrugged. 'No,' he said. 'A bit old-fashioned, but you can understand them.'

Pru breathed out and smiled. 'But there's nothing else *odd* about it?' she said.

'Well, it's in rhyme, of course,' said Jordy.

'I already said that,' said Sam.

'You did not!' Pru snapped.

'Sorry,' said Sam sheepishly. 'Is it important?'

Pru sighed. 'It confirms that we *are* dealing with Thomas Merson,' she said. She reached behind her for her notebook, flicked through and began reading.

' "When questioned about his idiosyncratic manner of speech, the accused replied as follows: 'Often witty, sometimes worse; Tom Tiddler only speaks in verse.' " Pru looked up again, and fiddled with the piece of paper in her hand. 'One more question,' she said finally. 'What do *you* think he wants?'

Sam shook his head. 'I can't work it out,' he said. 'He seems to be friendly. And he keeps mentioning something he wants to give me.' He pulled the wad of messages he'd copied down from his pocket, and looked through them. '*Help yourself to all that is his.* And again. *Until you have what you shall take.*'

Pru pursed her lips, thoughtfully. 'And you've no idea what it is?'

Jordy and Sam both answered at the same time.

'No,' said Jordy.

'Yes,' said Sam.

Pru looked at them both in turn. 'Well?' she said.

'He's told Sam that it's treasure,' said Jordy. 'But I'm not so sure. What better way is there to get a *boy* to do something, than get him chasing after treasure. It's like waving a carrot under a donkey's nose.'

'You didn't say that yesterday,' said Sam angrily.

'No, well . . .' said Jordy, looking down. 'I've been thinking. Who knows what we're going to unleash if we ever manage to open that box . . .'

'Box?' Pru jumped in. 'What box?'

Sam scowled. 'We found a strongbox up a tree.'

Pru breathed out noisily. 'After everything I said!' she exclaimed. 'I can't believe how lightly you're taking all this!'

'Lightly? Lightly? You don't know what it's like,' Sam shouted back. 'Nightmares, visions in mirrors, voices on the television, messages in the loft . . . If you want to know the truth, I'm terrified!' He looked down, and swallowed. '*I* don't know what's going on.'

Pru crouched down beside him. 'I'm sorry,' she said. 'We each have our own special way of dealing with the unknown.'

Sam looked up. 'I've *got* to trust him,' he said. 'Don't you see?'

Pru nodded. She sat back on the floor and crossed her legs. 'You said there were two Tom Tiddlers,' she said.

'Yes,' said Sam. 'That's the problem. One of

157

them seems really nice. The young one, with the beard,' he added looking up. 'He was the one I saw giving money to the poor children.'

'And the other one?' asked Pru.

Sam shuddered. 'He was horrible,' he said. 'Hardly human at all. But . . . I don't know. When I was in the bathroom,' he went on, 'they both appeared. But the young one sort of won. I think he's the *real* Tom Tiddler.' He looked up at Pru and smiled. 'The other one must just be in my imagination.'

'Unless it's the other way around,' said Pru dramatically. She held the piece of paper out in front of him. 'Is this what he looked like?'

Sam looked down. There on the page was a photograph of Tom Tiddler. Not, however, the smiling young man – this was a picture of the hideous dwarf in all his bandy-legged, hunch-backed, black-toothed, warty-nosed glory. The dark, suspicious eyes glared menacingly out of the photograph. Trembling with fear, Sam looked away.

'No!' he murmured. 'It can't be!'

CHAPTER THIRTY-ONE

When Sam showed no sign of reading the article, Pru took it back. Sam looked up. There were tears in his eyes. 'Sorry,' he sniffed. 'It was going all swimmy.'

'Shall I tell you what it says?' said Pru.

Sam nodded, and sniffed again.

'Right,' said Pru. 'It's an article written on the 23 November 1892 – nearly three weeks after Tom Tiddler died – and it looks back over the whole incident. He was released from prison on . . .' She glanced down at the paper. 'On 17 April, 1891.'

'His twenty-first birthday,' said Sam.

'Precisely,' said Pru. 'By this time,' she continued, 'Josiah Merson was dead and his

159

wife, Lucy, had long since gone away. Tom was homeless and alone. However,' she added, 'he was not, it seems, penniless. Apparently, unknown to his father, during his years of pick-pocketing, he had set aside a stash of his own. A sort of insurance. It was this money he used to construct the house in the centre of Wild Wood – and . . .' she paused. 'It was this money', she said, her voice suddenly low and hushed, 'which he used to lure little children.'

Sam shook his head. 'But he only wanted to help them,' he said.

'Did he, though?' said Pru. 'Or is that just what you're supposed to think? According to this', she said, and waved the paper in the air, 'his motives were altogether more sinister. They say that six children went missing.'

Sam felt his heart thumping in his chest. He rocked slowly backwards and forwards.

'Who knows what those long years behind bars did to the poor boy,' Pru continued. 'And then to be released, only to find that the person responsible for stealing his childhood had died. Not to mention the challenge of his height!' she said. 'All that pent-up rage!'

But Sam was not listening. He continued to rock – back and forwards, back and forwards. He simply wasn't able to believe what he'd just heard. Surely it couldn't be true.

'So what happened then?' asked Jordy.

Pru sighed. 'I'm afraid to say the fathers of the missing children, and their friends, decided to take the law into their own hands,' she said. 'Reprehensible, but understandable. They paid him a visit, so to speak, with cudgels and kerosene. They beat him . . .' she said quietly. 'And burned his body, along with the house.'

'And did they ever find the bodies of the children?' said Jordy.

'No,' said Pru. 'That was the awful thing . . .'

Suddenly, Sam stopped rocking. 'How does someone suddenly get a hump?' he said.

'Pardon?' said Pru.

'In the nightmare and the photo,' Sam said. 'He's got a hump. Where did it come from?'

'With age?' said Pru. 'Some senior citizens—'

'But Tom Tiddler wasn't old,' said Sam. 'And anyway, none of the original newspaper reports mention a hump. I mean, they would, wouldn't they – *if* he had one.'

Pru shrugged.

'Well, do they say that he's a dwarf?' Sam persisted.

'Yes,' said Pru, pursing her lips at the sound of the word. 'He stopped growing when he went to prison. Apparently he thought it was God's punishment for his life of crime.'

'But not the hump?' said Sam.

161

'Oh, for heaven's sake!' she said. 'They didn't need to mention it. You can see it clearly enough in the photograph. Look!'

Sam did look. He looked very carefully. Finally, he turned to Pru. 'But it isn't a photograph,' he said.

'What do you mean?'

'It's a drawing,' he said.

'Oh, nonsense,' said Pru. 'It's far too—'

'*An artist's impression of Tom Tiddler compiled from the descriptions of the eye-witnesses*,' Sam said, reading the miniscule caption at the side of the picture.

Pru snatched the piece of paper, and read it for herself. She looked up. 'You're right,' she said. 'But if they all described him in the same way, he must have had a hump.'

'Did he, though?' said Sam. 'Or is that just what you're supposed to think?'

Pru recognized her own words being quoted back at her. But she didn't understand. Why should the eyewitnesses have lied?

'Because they murdered him,' said Sam simply. 'You said so yourself. Don't you see? It was in their best interests to paint as hideous a picture as possible of their victim. More than that; it was what people *wanted* to believe.'

Pru nodded slowly. 'But how are we going to find out which one of us is right?'

'That's easy,' said Sam gravely. 'We wait.'

CHAPTER THIRTY-TWO

Saying it was one thing, doing it quite another. Sam glanced up at the classroom clock, and watched the second hand slowly groping its way up towards the twelve. The minute hand jumped forwards to join it. Three o'clock. It had been the fifth of November now for fifteen hours. So far, nothing had happened.

At sixteen hours, Sam and Jordy were just walking into Parkside Road. There was a firework display over the park later that evening which, since they still hadn't bought any fireworks of their own, they had decided to go and watch. Sam's parents had agreed to let him stay over at Jordy's.

At seventeen hours, they were picking at their

163

baked potatoes. Neither of them felt the least bit hungry.

At eighteen hours, the first rockets began hissing up into the sky. Every now and then, a banger exploded or a whizzer whined. Jordy made sure Rapper was safely locked up inside.

At nineteen hours, Sam and Jordy put on their scarves, gloves and hats. The display was due to start at half-past. Jordy slipped into her coat; Sam borrowed a donkey jacket from Pru, and at a quarter past seven, the pair of them left the house.

'Promise me you'll take care,' said Pru.

'We will,' said Jordy.

'Oh, this is ridiculous!' she said, the next instant. 'I can't possibly let you go up there on your own. Hang on a minute. I'll just get my cape . . .'

'No,' said Sam firmly. 'You mustn't come,' he said. 'It's got to be just us. He won't show up if he knows we've turned up with an adult. I know he won't.'

'But wouldn't that be better?' asked Pru.

Sam shook his head. 'And have to wait until next year?' he said. 'No way. This has to be sorted out tonight. Once and for all.'

Pru stared at him. 'I feel so helpless,' she said.

'We'll be fine,' Sam reassured her, as he swung the small rucksack up onto his back. 'We're only

164

going just over the road.' He laughed. 'Have you got any binoculars?'

'Yes,' said Pru, puzzled.

'Well, if you're really that worried,' said Sam, 'why don't you keep an eye on us?'

Pru's face broke into a grin. 'Good idea!' she said. 'I think I might just do that.'

Five minutes later, Sam and Jordy had crossed the grass to the roped-off top section of the park, where the fireworks had been set up. They – along with a couple of hundred others – stood waiting for the display to begin.

Sam glanced back at the house. 'Do you think she will be keeping an eye on us?' he said.

'I'm sure she'll try,' said Jordy. 'Though it won't be easy – not with all these people. Still,' she added, 'safety in numbers, eh? If anything happens, we'll just shout for help . . .'

Behind them, Jordy and Sam heard a sudden *whoosh* as the first rocket of the display flew like an arrow up into the sky.

'Hooray!' everyone yelled. And, as it burst into shower after shower of gold and silver, their cheers turned to one long *aaaaah*!

The next instant, a volley of rockets went up, lighting the darkness with an explosion of changing colours. Banging, crackling, whistling. Now red, now green, now deepest blue. It was as if an unseen hand was tossing precious stones from the heavens. Rubies, emeralds, sapphires. Diamonds and pearls. Untold wealth, tumbling down from the sky.

Open-mouthed with wonder, Sam and Jordy stared, mesmerized by the ever-changing combinations of colour. At first they didn't notice that the bangs and crackles were becoming more muffled, the whistles fading away. Entranced by what they could see, they did not even think about what they could no longer hear.

It wasn't until the voice broke through the silence, that they realized just how quiet it had become. And by then, it was too late. Not only were Sam and Jodie unable to hear the *oohs* and *aahs* of the people around them, they were also unable to make themselves heard. It was as if an invisible soundproofed wall had encircled the pair of them, shutting them in and cutting them off. Only the voice – the high-pitched nasal voice – managed to penetrate the cocooning silence.

> 'The time has come, the end is near,
> Tom Tiddler must soon disappear.
> The end is near, the time has come,
> To clear my name – for a tidy sum.'

Without even pausing to wonder what the words might mean, Sam and Jordy found themselves leaving the firework display. The time had arrived, Tom Tiddler had called, and they had no choice but to obey.

Pru's heart missed a beat as she watched the two children emerging from the crowd and walking, zombie-like, towards the trees. She laid the binoculars down, hurried out of her study and downstairs.

'I *knew* I shouldn't have let them go on their own,' she muttered to herself, over and over. 'I just knew it!'

She picked up the phone and dialled 999. Then she called the Dillons. Finally, having switched the answer-machine on, she grabbed her coat, ran outside to the car and skidded off in a shower of gravel.

They must have gone to that clearing where I found Sam, she thought. I just pray I'm not too late!

CHAPTER THIRTY-THREE

Jordy kept close to Sam as they walked on through the trees. She knew that he had seen it all before. This was the forest he had described in such detail, with its dense dirty undergrowth, its greasy grimy evergreen leaves, its bare branches that now scratched and scraped at both their faces.

On and on they went; deeper and deeper into the forest. Finally, just as Jordy was beginning to give up hope, they arrived at the gate in the picket fence. Sam pushed it open, and entered the circular garden.

Jordy followed him nervously. She looked round at the abundant display of flowers, fruits and vegetables spilling over from the outer ring.

Chickens, which had been roosting in the apple trees, left their perches, flew down and began scratching at the earth between the planks of wood. A cockerel, standing on the roof of Tom Tiddler's simple house, raised its head and flapped its wings.

'Cock-a-doodle-doo!' it crowed. 'Cock-a-doodle-doo!'

As the bird continued its urgent cry, Jordy and Sam heard another noise. It was the sound of unoiled hinges creaking open. They looked up to see the gap in the doorway slowly widening. A beady eye peeked out from the shadows.

'Tom Tiddler!' Sam called. 'We have come.'

There was silence from inside the house. The eye continued to stare.

'Tom Tiddler!' he called again.

Finally, the door opened right up, and Tom Tiddler stood there: hairy, warty, bandy and hunched. Jordy screamed and turned away. The hideous creature sighed and turned to Sam. The boy stared back defiantly.

'You can't hurt *me*!' he said bravely.

Tom Tiddler shook his head.

'A childlike mind, a childish frame –
You've listened to their lies again!'

Jordy tugged at Sam's sleeve. 'Let's get out of here,' she said. .

But Sam was not about to leave. Not now. 'What do you mean?' he said.

'A childish frame, a childlike mind,'
Tom Tiddler continued.
'Always inquisitive, never unkind!'

Sam frowned. 'Their lies.' But who were *they*? The so-called eyewitnesses, perhaps? Or maybe Pru, who had filled their heads with doubts and fears about the little man . . . The trouble was, it was so difficult to work out the precise meaning of Tom Tiddler's verses.

Sam found himself growing impatient. 'Do you have to talk in riddles the whole time?' he snapped.

The ugly hunchback squinted back at him. Sam felt as if he was looking at a scared, mistrustful animal rather than a man.

'It's all right,' he said, more softly now. 'I do believe you . . .'

The creature jerked its head towards Jordy, who was still standing with her back turned.

'Jordy,' said Sam. 'Look again. But remember this time, he wants to help us. Not harm us.'

Jordy looked up tearfully. 'Are you sure?' she whispered.

Sam nodded. 'If that's what we want,' he said.

Head down, Jordy turned right around.

'Come on,' said Sam. 'Help, not harm.'

Jordy raised her head slowly, until she found herself staring at Tom Tiddler. She smiled.

'You see,' said the bearded young man, 'everything is not always what is seems.'

'But . . .' said Jordy.

Tom Tiddler raised his hand to silence her. 'There is much to say. And so little time.'

'So you *don't* always have to speak in rhyme,' said Sam and, realizing that he himself had done just that, burst out laughing. 'It must be contagious!'

Tom Tiddler smiled. 'No,' he said. 'The riddling rhymes are not necessary. But adults find them irritating,' he added, with a grin. 'And children – usually – find them enchanting, enticing . . .'

Jordy's eyes narrowed suspiciously. If the verses had only served to gain their interest, perhaps she had been right about the *treasure*, too. What if he had lied? What if that, too, was just a way of enchanting and enticing children?

Tom Tiddler turned towards her. Like a mask, the repulsive face of the creature hovered over his pleasant features. Jordy looked down guiltily.

'Jordy!' said Sam. 'Stop it!'

'I can't help it,' she cried. 'Why should I believe him? It was in all the papers, what he did!'

'But it wasn't true!' said Sam. He turned back to Tom Tiddler. The mask had disappeared. 'Tell

171

her!' he demanded. 'Tell her what really happened.'

Tom Tiddler nodded. 'I owe you both an explanation,' he said. 'Though some things you already know. While others . . .' he sighed, 'I scarcely understand myself.

'I picked my first pocket when I was a babe in arms,' he began. 'My mother had handed me to a lady about to travel on the stagecoach to London. I flung my arms around her neck, and slipped her silk handkerchief from her sleeve under my shawl. My mother and father were overjoyed when they discovered it. They showered me in kisses. I learnt that day that love had to be paid for.

'The years went by, and I became the finest pickpocket the country has ever seen. Wallets and purses, lockets and chains, necklaces, bracelets – even rings were not safe from my nimble fingers. Once, I even stole a man's braces off his very back – simply because I could.

'My parents were happy. They would pawn the goods and spend the money on beer, returning drunk, at two in the morning, to drink the health of their diligent son. Life was good, for one who had known no other . . .

'Until, that is, the accident,' he said, and he winced at the memory. He looked up. There were tears in his eyes.

'A horse kicked Tom Tiddler,' he said. 'It broke

his leg. Three months, he had to remain in bed . . .'

He paused, and turned to Sam. 'Yes,' he said. 'In the room which now is yours.'

'So what happened?' said Jordy.

'Happened?' he said dully. 'They called Tom Tiddler idle. They beat him for his laziness . . .' He looked down. 'When he recovered, Tom Tiddler saw his parents through different eyes. Now, when he went out robbing, he put a little bit aside for himself; squirrelled away for a rainy day.

'Time passed, but though Tom's fingers were as nimble as ever, his leg had never fully recovered. On that fateful Tuesday morning, when the toff with the monocle shouted "thief!", Tom Tiddler was not able to run away fast enough.'

'And they sent you to prison,' said Sam.

Tom Tiddler nodded. 'But that was not all he had to endure. For God, too, had decided to punish Tom Tiddler. And what a punishment it was!

'From the moment the prison door slammed shut, I never grew so much as a fraction of an inch. As I scratched the passing months on the wall by my bed, I came to understand that I had to atone for my crimes, or else remain for ever imprisoned inside the body of a child.'

'And that's why you gave the money and

173

jewellery to the boys and girls,' said Sam. 'To make you grow taller.'

'No,' he said, sadly. 'By then I was twenty-one. I knew I was never going to grow any more. And yet, the idea of giving away my riches had been a good one, and would not leave me . . .' He paused. 'I understood what the children were going through, you see. I wanted to help them. And I did . . . for a while.'

His eyes misted over again.

'Somehow, their parents got to hear about Tom Tiddler – I suppose one of the children must have been careless. One night, I heard the distant echo of beery voices and heavy feet coming through the forest.' He stopped and listened.

'But I can hear them now!' said Jordy.

Tom Tiddler nodded. 'They are coming for me now,' he said. 'Coming to kill the goose that laid the golden eggs.' He smiled. 'But they will never find what they are looking for.'

Sam looked over his shoulder nervously. The sound of the approaching men was getting louder. There was still something he had to find out. He turned back to Tom Tiddler.

'But why me?' he said.

The little man shook his head. 'I said there were things I do not understand,' he said. 'Maybe because you sleep in the room where Tom Tiddler once lay. I cannot say. All I know is that

I was roused from my sleep by a smell. A curious smell. The sweetness of innocence, soured by the burden of adult concerns too complex to comprehend.'

Sam frowned. He didn't understand. And still, the men were getting nearer.

'What do you mean?' he said.

'I mean,' said Tom Tiddler, sharply, 'that childhood is sacred. It is holy. And no parent on this earth has the right to deprive their sons and daughters of it.'

His face flushed with anger and indignation, Tom Tiddler fell silent. He glanced over at the trees. Sam stared at him.

'So, I did call you,' he said. 'Not the other way around.'

Tom Tiddler turned back and looked him in the eyes. 'Let us simply say that I was there to answer your cries for help,' he said. He nodded back at the trees. 'They will be here soon,' he said. 'There is something I must still do.'

With those words, he reached inside his coat. Sam froze. It was the moment he had already lived through twice. As the hand re-emerged, Sam saw it held something long and silver; something that glinted in the moonlight.

He gasped. Then he blinked. All at once, he saw the object for what it was. Not a knife. But a key.

'Take it,' said Tom Tiddler. 'You know what it

is for. Use it wisely. Use it well.' He turned to Jodie. 'And see that the world learns the truth about Tom Tiddler. I am not a monster.'

'But what about the children?' said Jordy. 'What happened to them?'

'The ones I showed you,' said Tom Tiddler, turning to Sam. '*Nothing* happened to them. They were merely the excuse for their fathers to rob and murder. Soon after – one by one – the parents "found" their missing children.'

'Why didn't they tell anyone they were alive?' said Jordy.

'They did,' said Tom Tiddler. 'But by then it was too late. The rumours and lies had taken root: everyone seemed to know of a friend of a friend whose child had been slain by the hideous wicked dwarf. And in time, even the children began to believe the tales they heard.'

At that moment, the first of the men burst out of the undergrowth. Jordy and Sam looked round in horror.

'Go!' said Tom Tiddler urgently. 'You *must* leave, now!'

'But what about you?' said Sam.

'What happened has happened,' said Tom Tiddler. 'Only the future concerns me now. And that, Sam and Jordy, is in your hands. Now, run! Get out of this place! They are coming for me *and* you!'

Without waiting to hear what he meant by

that, Jordy and Sam took to their heels. They ran round the back of the house, dashed across the path and flower-beds and vaulted over the fence. As she landed on the far side, Jordy's foot went over on its side.

'Aaii!' she yelped, and fell to the ground.

Sam stopped and pulled her out of sight behind a thick bush. While Jordy rubbed at her tender ankle, Sam peeked through the trees.

It was difficult to make out exactly what was going on. The yellow glow of swinging lanterns sent crazy shadows bouncing off the branches of the trees. There were raised voices; muffled, angry – and the sound of banging and crashing. And above it all, the strident voice of Tom Tiddler, ringing through the air.

'What are you after? What do you need? Do I detect the whiff of greed? What do you n . . .'

Suddenly the voice fell silent. The pungent smell of kerosene wafted towards them. Sam turned to Jordy. 'We can't stay here,' he said. 'Do you think you can walk?'

'With a bit of help,' she said.

Sam took Jordy's hand and pulled her to her feet. 'Come on,' he said. 'Let's get out of here.'

Half-hopping, half-walking, Sam and Jordy hobbled through the woods, putting as much distance between them and Tom Tiddler's Ground as they could. They hadn't gone more than fifty metres when a sudden WOOF filled the air. A blast of scorching heat shoved them in the back and sent them sprawling to the ground.

Sam looked round. The sky above the trees was tinged with orange. But not, he realized, from a burning fire. It was the glow from the street lamps in the town.

'We made it,' he said. 'We're back in the present.' He looked down at his clenched fist, and opened it slowly. There in his palm was the key. 'And so is the . . .'

'Sssh!' said Jordy. 'I can hear something.'

Sam looked round. 'I can't . . .'

'SSSH!'

Sam listened. Jordy was right. There *was* something. He could heard a car in low gear, approaching from the left; then another, from the right. Dazzling headlights flashed from between the trees.

Jordy turned to Sam. ' "They're coming for me *and* you," – that's what Tom Tiddler said. He must have known.'

'But who are they?' said Sam.

'I don't know,' said Jordy. 'And what's more, I don't intend to find out.'

CHAPTER THIRTY-FOUR

Jordy and Sam had just reached the tree when, suddenly, a loud crash echoed through the woods.

'What on earth was that?' said Jordy.

'I don't know,' said Sam.

'Do you think it could have been Pru? If she saw us leaving the firework display . . . Maybe we should go and see.'

All at once, a cold wind whistled through the trees. It encircled the two children and spun round and round them, tugging at their coats and flicking their scarves and hair into their eyes. And as it blew, Jordy and Sam heard an all-too-familiar voice.

'NO!' it howled.

Jordy looked at Sam and swallowed. 'On the other hand,' she said, 'maybe not!'

Sam nodded. 'We'll check *after* we've seen what's in the box,' he said.

This time, after Jordy had helped Sam up to the first branch, he turned, leant down and pulled Jordy up beside him. Since they hadn't been able to agree who should open the strongbox, they had decided that they should *both* climb up to inspect it.

A couple of minutes later, the pair of them were standing next to the 'fork that never graced a table', looking down at the silver strongbox. Jordy shone her torch down on it. The trunk had all but swallowed up the box.

'You can see why I couldn't move it,' said Sam.

Jordy nodded. 'Look,' she said, pointing to two rusting letters scratched into the metal above the lock.

'T.T.,' said Sam, and smiled. He took the key from his pocket and, holding the little oval cover to one side, inserted it in the lock. Despite being there for over a century, when Sam turned the key, the mechanism clicked open as if it had been oiled only the day before.

Sam turned to Jordy. 'Come on, then,' he said.

Jordy leant forward and grasped the top of the box.

'Now,' said Sam.

Together, they both lifted. The lid rose up and

rested back on its hinges. So far, so good! No imprisoned ghoul or ghastly ghost emerged – at least, none they could see. Sam and Jordy looked inside. Sam laughed, and reached in.

'What's that?' asked Jordy.

Sam held the dangly straps up in the air, and shone his torch at them. 'Braces,' he said.

'Braces?' said Jordy.

'He said he'd taken a pair off a man,' Sam laughed. 'I suppose this is proof of just how good he was at his *job*.'

'I can think of better proof!' said Jordy. 'What else have we got?'

'Some scarves,' said Sam, pulling at a red and gold square of silk.

As he tugged it, the scarf began to unravel. 'Mind!' said Jordy. 'There's something inside.'

While Sam pointed his torch in her direction, Jordy carefully unwrapped the layers of silk. As the last piece unfolded, something sparkled brightly in the beam of light. Jordy gasped.

'Earrings,' she said excitedly. 'And they look like diamonds!'

In the next scarf was an emerald brooch. In the next, a ruby-encrusted locket on a gold chain. In the one after that, a small leather wallet containing a dozen *penny black* stamps. And so it went on. Each of the silk scarves was wrapped around a separate item that Tom Tiddler had stashed away. Watches, sovereigns, bracelets and rings; phials of perfume and strings of pearls. It was a treasure chest that dreams are made of. And Sam and Jordy – with a little help from Tom Tiddler – had found it.

They arrived back at Jordy's house to find all the lights on. Two cars were parked in the driveway: Pru's and a panda car. What was more, the front of both of them was damaged.

'Do you think they crashed into each other?' said Jordy.

Sam shrugged.

'If they were both heading for the clearing . . .'

At that moment, the door flew open.

'Mum!' said Sam in astonishment.

'Oh, Sam, you're safe!' she cried and hurried towards him. 'I've been so worried.'

'I'm all right,' said Sam. 'We both are.' He looked at Jordy, and grinned. 'And we've got something to show you.'

You could have heard a pin drop as Sam and Jordy removed bundle after bundle from their backpacks, unfolded them and laid them gently down on the dining-room table. Neither Pru, nor Pete and Sally; not even the two constables had ever come so close to so much wealth.

'The treasure,' said Pru finally.

Sam nodded. 'I told you he was all right.'

Sam's mum was looking from one to the other.

182

Finally she could stand it no more. 'Would *someone* mind telling me what's going on!'

Sam turned and looked at her. She looked tired. 'I wanted to tell you before,' he said awkwardly. 'But you and Dad were . . . had . . .'

'Tell me now,' said his mum gently.

Sam took a deep breath. 'It all started with that nightmare . . .' he began. It felt good telling his parents everything that had been happening. And by the time he came to the bit about unlocking the treasure box, he was positively enjoying recounting the story. Trust his mum to put a dampener on things!

'The thing is,' she said, 'this Tom Tiddler was a thief. The treasure is all stolen. It has to be returned to its original owners.' She turned to the police constables. 'Am I right?'

Before either of them had a chance to reply, the window burst open and an icy blast flew round the room.

'NO!' bellowed the voice for a second time.

'What on earth was that?' said one of the constables looking round.

'That's him,' said Jordy. '*That's* Tom Tiddler.'

'But . . .' said *all* the grown-ups together. The next moment they were silenced, as the voice boomed out.

'Tom Tiddler I was, Tom Tiddler I am.
My treasure belongs to Jordy and Sam.

Tom Tiddler I am, Tom Tiddler I was.
Ask me why and I'll answer "because"!'

Before any of them could speak, the voice
continued. This time, not only in Pru's living
room, but also on every radio and every
television in every home in Banworth.

'A hundred years have come and gone,
Tom Tiddler finds it strange;
When everything is said and done,
There's been so little change.'

Inside rooms all over the town, people were
looking at each other. Who was speaking? What
did it mean?

The voice continued:

'Poverty still eats at us,
Like a small but hungry weevil.
The love of money is bad indeed,
But the lack of it is evil.'

EPILOGUE

What the taller of the two constables was about to explain, when he was so abruptly interrupted by Tom Tiddler, was this. Although the items *were* stolen property, since they had gone missing so long ago, there was no chance of them being returned to their rightful owners. Once three months had elapsed with no-one claiming the items, they legally became Jordy and Sam's property.

Finally, Tom Tiddler had achieved what he had set out to achieve.

When it came to the auction, the treasure raised close on a million pounds – for Sam and Jordy, an impossible amount of money to comprehend.

Jordy, who had always fancied herself in a rock band, bought an electric guitar. Sam bought himself a new jacket and a mountain bike, as well as a car for his dad. Not that he had needed to. Shortly after the fateful Firework Night, his dad had landed a brilliant new job at I.C.C.'s – a computer software manufacturer. His mum's situation also changed for the better; she was made manageress of the off-licence. Like Sam's nightmares, the sound of his parents' furious arguments had become a thing of the past. Life was definitely, as his dad liked to say, 'on the up'.

As for the rest of the money; half they gave away – to Children in Need – and half they 'squirrelled away for a rainy day'. They *thought* Tom Tiddler would approve – but they couldn't be sure. Since that final broadcast, he had remained completely silent.

Easter came and went and, to Sam's delight, Jordy did not move away. Pru could see how happy her granddaughter was in Banworth, and had decided to stay. They used some of the money to put a deposit down on the house. As for the book of children's games she had been researching, Pru finished the final version in February. Since the newspapers had been full of 'Tom Tiddler' stories since the discovery of the treasure, the book was printed in record time. *Nuts in May* by Prudence Carraway was published – appropriately enough – on May 1st.

It became an instant hit. Though, to be honest, most people who bought the book only read the section which started on page 182 and ended on page 206: the section about Tom Tiddler's Ground.

'Agnes Sharples, Thomas Willoughby, Edwin Marwood, Eliza Bates, Mildred Bingham and John (Jack) Coleridge – these are the six children Tom Tiddler was supposed to have murdered. Having tracked down their death certificates, I can confirm that all of them outlived Thomas "Tiddler" Merson, some by many decades,' Sam read out. 'There is only one conclusion to draw from the evidence: Tom Tiddler was innocent of all the charges laid against him. This particular bogeyman of the game *Tom Tiddler's Ground* never deserved to become so. He didn't harm children, he only ever helped them.' Sam closed the book and smiled. 'I hope *he* knows,' he said.

'I'm sure he does,' said Jordy.

That night, Sam had a dream. A wonderful dream. He was standing in a playground with lots of other children. A chalk circle had been drawn on the tarmac.

'Here we are in Tom Tiddler's Ground
Picking up gold and silver!' they cried.

But no-one was frightened now. No-one was

187

running screaming away from the monstrous *it*. Instead, the air was filled with the sound of laughing and giggling, as the boys and girls skipped round and round in a big circle. At the centre was a small young man with bright blue eyes and a beard. He, too, was laughing.

Suddenly, the ring broke open. Tom Tiddler left the circle and started walking towards a bright light. He paused for a second, turned and sought out Sam with his eyes. He smiled, waved and turned back to the light. The next minute, he was gone.

Sam woke, still full of the dream. He ran downstairs and was just about to pick up the receiver, when the telephone rang.

'Hello?' said a voice.

'Jordy?' said Sam. 'I was just—'

'Sam, I've just had the most amazing dream,' she said. 'He's—'

'—all right,' said Sam. 'I know. He said goodbye to me, too.'

THE END

THE MIDNIGHT HAND
Paul Stewart

Something is out there . . .

At the stroke of midnight, as a huge bronze bell tolls the hours, something stirs in a dark and narrow recess. A hand. A skeletal hand with a monstrous awareness of a long ago tragedy . . .

Tom, newly arrived at Styles Grange boarding school, is awakened on his very first night by the creepy feeling of something stroking his face. Then suddenly, scuttling into the shadows under his bed, is . . . a severed hand!

A bloodcurdling nightmare of a tale from a master of suspense.

'A truly creepy story with moments of pure terror . . . gripping'
1015, The Times

0 440 86348 1

CORGI YEARLING BOOKS

From the Carnegie Medal winning author

INSIDE THE WORM
Robert Swindells

*The worm was close now. So close Fliss
could smell the putrid stench of its breath.
Its slavering jaws gaped to engulf her . . .*

Everyone in Elsworth knows the local
legend about the monstrous worm that once
terrorized the village. But it never *really*
happened. Or did it? For when Fliss and her
friends are chosen to re-enact the legend
for the village Festival, something
very sinister begins to happen.

Hidden within the framework of the worm
costume, the four who are to play the part of
the worm dance as one across the ground.
And Fliss begins to feel real fear. Somehow
the worm itself is returning – with a
thousand-year hunger in its belly,
and vengeance in its brain . . .

0 440 86300 7

CORGI YEARLING BOOKS

THE GHOST DOG
Pete Johnson

*'I sensed hot breath on my neck. It was right
behind me. It'll get me, I must run faster . . .
faster . . .'*

Only mad scientists in stories can create
monsters, can't they? Not ten-year-old boys
like Daniel. Well, not until the night of his
spooky party when he and his friends make
up a ghost story about a terrifying dog . . .

It's a story made up to frighten Aaron –
tough, big-headed Aaron. But to Dan's
horror, what begins as a ghost story turns
into a nightmare. Each night the ghost dog
– a bloodthirsty, howling monster – haunts
his dreams, and Dan suspects that what he
conjured up with his imagination has
somehow become . . . real!

**WINNER OF THE 1997 YOUNG
TELEGRAPH/FULLY BOOKED AWARD**

0 440 86341 4

CORGI YEARLING BOOKS

CLOCKWORK
or ALL WOUND UP
Philip Pullman

*Tick, tock, tick, tock! Some stories are like
that. Once you've wound them up,
nothing will stop them . . .*

A tormented apprentice clock-maker – and a
deadly knight in armour. A mechanical
prince – and the sinister Dr Kalmenius,
who some say is the devil . . . Wind up these
characters, fit them into a story on a cold
winter's evening, with the snow swirling
down, and suddenly life and the
story begin to merge in a peculiarly
macabre – and unstoppable – way.

Almost like clockwork . . .

**'Exciting, scary, romantic and
deliciously readable'**
The Guardian

SILVER MEDAL WINNER, SMARTIES
AWARD IN 1997
SHORTLISTED FOR THE CARNEGIE
MEDAL IN 1997

0 440 863430

CORGI YEARLING BOOKS